CRISIS GAME

CRISIS GAME

A Novel of the Cold War

by

Craig Eisendrath

First Fiction Series

SUNSTONE
PRESS

SANTA FE

© 2002 by Craig Eisendrath. All rights reserved.

Printed and bound in the United States of America. No part of this book may be reproduced in any form or by any electronic or mechanical means including information storage and retrieval systems without permission in writing from the publisher, except by a reviewer who may quote brief passages in a review.

Sunstone books may be purchased for educational, business, or sales promotional use. For information please write: Special Markets Department, Sunstone Press, P.O. Box 2321, Santa Fe, New Mexico 87504-2321.

FIRST EDITION

10 9 8 7 6 5 4 3 2 1

Library of Congress Cataloging-in-Publication Data:

Eisendrath, Craig R.
    Crisis game: a novel of the Cold War / by Craig Eisendrath. —1st ed.
        p. cm.
    ISBN 0-86534-332-2 — ISBN 0-86534-333-0 (pbk.)
    1. Cold War—Fiction. I. Title.
    PS3605 .I84 C75 2002
    813' .54—dc21   2001049537

Published in

SUNSTONE PRESS
Post Office Box 2321
Santa Fe, NM 87504-2321 / USA
(505) 988-4418 / *orders only* (800) 243-5644
FAX (505) 988-1025
www.sunstonepress.com

For Roberta

PREFACE

In the late 1960s, at the height of the Cold War with the Soviet Union, the United States faced an enemy that could destroy most of its population and render its territory a nuclear waste. One false step might launch thermonuclear terror.

To prepare our diplomatic and strategic personnel to avoid such a step, and emerge the winner, the U.S. government contracted with think tanks and universities to structure crisis games. These games allowed the players to try out moves in situations which, while not real, were close enough to mimic genuine crises. The results were studied by officials of the State Department, Department of Defense, and other agencies, and influenced diplomatic and military decisions.

Not only did these games have rules like any other game, such as chess or poker, but their managers sent the players a steady stream of communiqués—usually telegrams and intelligence reports—that resembled those they might receive in an actual crisis. Some might report the detection of possible missile launches; others, suspicious military or diplomatic moves; still others, the assessment of the motives of foreign diplomats and statesmen. The question always remained: How would the players' counterparts react to similar communiqués in a real crisis?

As these games were being played, the players, who were diplomatic and military personnel, academics, and politicians, continued their normal lives in the Washington world.

While the situations and characters presented in CRISIS GAME are not intended to depict specific situations or persons, the game presented in this novel was inspired by games being played in Washington when I was a young Foreign Service Officer in the Department of State.

—Craig Eisendrath
Philadelphia, 2001

THE RULES

■ The game is designed to simulate as closely as possible the conditions of a crisis in international affairs. Players who have had operational experience will find most of the procedures familiar.

"So glad to meet you, Mrs. Klein.

Anne Sansone shaped a waxy smile as she stood, perfectly composed, in the midst of the cocktail party. It was not that she fitted in that well with the period furniture that lined the walls here in the Charles Francis Adams Room of the Department of State. What impressed Catherine Klein was Anne's confident ruthlessness—she reminded Catherine of Lady Bird Johnson.

"I guess in the next few weeks we won't be seeing too much of our husbands," Anne said.

"Because of the game?"

"The Senator's never played one, but I understand it can be quite demanding, almost as if it were a real crisis."

"But, of course, it's not," Catherine said. "It's just the kind of thing—well, isn't it?—that men do when they want to feel important, and there's not enough important things for them to do."

Anne Sansone looked away.

"Michael, my husband—you've met him, haven't you?" Catherine went on. "He's practically convinced himself it's actually happening."

"What?"

Anne must regularly go to a hairdresser, she was so perfect. Catherine never went to them; prided herself on her Radcliffe sloppiness.

"The game, the whole idea," Catherine persisted.

"I forget, just what part does your husband play?"

"He's a law professor," Catherine replied, "so I suppose it's something legal."

"He'll probably find it quite stimulating."

"I'm sure he will."

A barrel-chested man signaled to Anne from across the room. "Coming, Frank. So nice to have met you, my dear. We must get together sometime, now that we're all in this together." Anne Sansone disappeared in a swish of silk.

■ **Communications may be questioned by players among themselves, but they may not be discussed with Control or countermanded. Reality must be dealt with as presented.**

"It's all so interesting, don't you think?" asked Betty Holmes. Her open, blue eyes were those of a little girl. She must be in her seventies.

"The game?" asked Catherine Klein.

"When Stoddard heard he'd been chosen as a player I think he was, well, you know, he's not a very demonstrative person, but I think he was interested, though maybe intrigued is a better word.

I'm never quite sure with him what he feels, even after all these years. Yes, intrigued, that *must* be the word."

Catherine smiled. "It *sounds* right."

"Do you really think so?"

"It is if it says what you want it to say."

"That's the point. I'm never quite sure, at least with Stoddard." Betty looked up at the ceiling. "Do you ever have that problem, not knowing what words mean?"

"Occasionally."

"It's the bane of my life."

"The bane of your life?" Catherine asked.

"So much of life, my dear, is lost in semantic confusion. If we could only use words with greater precision, so many of life's problems would disappear, just like clouds." Betty Holmes sighed. "I've tried to discuss these ideas with Stoddard, but he isn't as interested in them as I feel he should be. It's so very important, I mean, semantic confusion. It can cause so much unhappiness, not only among people but among nations."

"I'm sure it does."

"Stoddard does tend to be quite precise. That's why he was such an effective diplomat—he retired, you know, just last year. And now he's threatening to return to his boyhood home in Elton, Massachusetts, but, thank God, he keeps putting it off. I think it's for my sake, the dear. He knows, he must know, I would just *die* in a backwater like Elton. I mean, what would I do with myself there month after month?"

"I haven't any idea."

"And yet Stoddard continues to mention it. Perhaps it's just his way of teasing me. Do you think so?" The older woman actually squeezed Catherine's hand. "It would be too hard, too hard after all those years abroad. All those years in the limelight, you might say, years we shared together in foreign capitals."

"Did you enjoy them?"

"Oh yes, more than I can say. Some women complain about what they call the ardures of being a Foreign Service wife, but I never did. I loved that life. I guess I have a certain flair for it. There's nothing I'd rather do than prepare a dinner for a whole flock of fascinating people. I even liked memorizing guest lists. It was sort of like high school Latin, which was all memory, and I was rather good at *that*, too—it was my one medal. We were Episcopal, but my parents sent me to a Catholic school, which is how I happened to take Latin at an early age. One of life's little accidents. Did you ever study Latin?"

"Actually, I didn't."

"What was I saying? Yes, it was about Latin. But what was the Latin about? Oh yes, about dinner parties. Some of the younger Foreign Service wives used to complain about having to give them, but I never minded, not at all. Now it's almost as if Stoddard were back in it."

"So you won't be returning to Elton, at least for a while?"

"No, mercifully no. It's—is that the right word, someone said you were a poet so you must be painfully conscious of the right word—is it a reprieve?" Betty Holmes caught sight of a tall, elegant figure. "Oh, Manse, Mansefield Vane, you *must* come over here and meet my new friend, Catherine Klein."

Dowdy, was that the right word? Catherine Klein asked herself, or was it nondescript? But did everything in the world, even Betty Holmes, deserve description? Was that a sign of greatness of spirit, that one made no such distinctions? Michael always said she was a snob, but look how *he* was sidling up to her to meet Mansefield Vane.

"Mr. Vane, this is my husband, Michael," Catherine said.

She noted that they were dressed rather alike, as if Vane's tailor—he must go to a tailor—had, after all the fitting and mysterium of his craft, virtually duplicated Brooks Brothers. She had always told

Michael that he looked distinguished in his Brooks Brothers suits, but now, next to Mansefield Vane, he looked merely uncomfortable. She had once hoped he would dress like Einstein with big sweaters and baggy pants, and be absorbed in matters which had no immediate edge of success.

"I've already had the pleasure, at the briefing this afternoon." Vane almost bowed. "Mr. Klein will be my Legal Advisor, a role which, I'm sure, you will play with distinction."

"I'll do my best," Klein said.

Vane was all verticals. What was the Renaissance proportion, Catherine asked herself, between the head and the body?

"That is all one can ask a lawyer to do," Vane remarked. "Whether one wins or loses must also depend, at least in part, on the strength of one's case."

"I'm always impressed by how little," Klein said. "It's a consideration which gives us lawyers some moral pause."

"Quite so."

"We play our part in a triumvirate of judge, prosecution, and defense."

Catherine had heard this one of Michael's before.

"And you are necessarily the defense?" Vane asked him.

"Probably."

"Were I concerned with litigation—my practice has always been of a rather different sort—I should like to try judging, although I suspect all that magisterial frippery."

"It does become grating," Klein said.

"I should like a little more recognition of what must eventually be recognized as the propensity of judges for human error."

"It would help."

Vane smiled, as if to himself. "A pleasure, Mr. Klein. We shall be at it rather early tomorrow, if my hunch is correct, although I have nothing definite on this to set a watch by." He extended his hand. "Mrs. Holmes, Mrs. Klein?"

■ Moves of the President need not be cleared with other members of the team. Relations of authority, precedent, and prestige between team players are those normally prevailing in the U.S. Government.

"You know, of course, that was *the* Mansefield Vanc," Klein told his wife when they had a moment alone.

"And it thrills you."

"That's a little strong. But it is exciting. I've always been enormously interested in the man—I've heard him speak, of course. And now we'll be working together. Yes, it *is* exciting."

"What? The aura of power?"

"Catherine, are you accusing me of being a sycophant?"

"I think you are interested in power like some people are interested in knowledge, or some other people are interested in beauty, or ..."

"Let's have this discussion later." He looked quickly around but didn't see anyone he could easily turn to. "The President isn't here. I thought that would be still another treat for you."

"Who's the President again?"

"I told you—Mitchell Murray. Didn't you really remember?"

"I honestly didn't."

"Getting him in the game must have been quite a coup for Control. Murray's still an immensely powerful man, though, of course, having lost the election, his power right now would be difficult to define."

"Who's Control, Michael?"

"The people running the game."

"So who are they?"

"I *said* they were the people running the game. They're probably some think tank or other. I don't think it was discussed in the briefing."

"Aren't you just a bit curious?"

"Well, I suppose I'll find out. It never actually crossed my mind."

"So then you don't know. If you don't find out now, you'll forget. You always forget what I ask you to do."

"There's Senator Sansone. I need to talk to him, okay? I'll be back in a minute."

■ **Knowledge of other players and teams will be that which players might reasonably assume in real operations. For biographic information about members of the American or other teams, players may wish to consult Biographic Intelligence in the Administration Office.**

"So, Mr. Klein, how do you size up this situation we're supposed to be in?"

Senator Frank Sansone bulked out in front of him, as Klein imagined senators had in an earlier day, the Daniel Websters and Thomas Hart Bentons of the world, with their oratorical chests, their sense of solidity. Warren Harding had also looked like a senator, and had carried, as did Sansone, the taint of corruption. Hadn't Sansone been tied up with Nick D'Antonio, the mobster, with that whole New Jersey mafia? Klein half remembered, yet couldn't think of anything specific, just an association. Again, the oratorical image filled the space.

"Well, my feeling," Klein said, "is that we should seek a multilateral solution. Any attempt we might make to impose a solution ourselves would get us into still another situation like Vietnam, which is exactly what I think we should want to avoid."

"Very interesting."

"That's the point of the game, don't you think?"

" You may be right."

"A couple of months ago," Klein told him, "I published an article which anticipates exactly, *exactly*, the kind of situation we're supposed to be in right now, and proposes a multilateral solution as a way of diffusing responsibility and blunting antagonisms. The . . ."

"So you see a UN role in all this?"

"Of course, the United Nations would be the agency to handle it."

"Well, the next few weeks the UN will be *my* concern, Klein, so I'm pleased you see it this way." Sansone looked him right in the eyes. "If I got some UN action under way, could I count on your support?"

"If you'd like to see my article, I think it might prove helpful."

"Yes, I'd like to very much."

"Maybe we *could* work together."

"Yes, Klein, I think we can." Sansone turned and surveyed the room. "Klein, it's hard to believe this is just a game. Just look at the people they've got here, people I've worked with for years, I mean *real* people. It's amazing!"

"I hope you're including yourself," Klein added quickly. "It's a *Who's Who.*"

"Yes. What did you say you did?"

"I'm a law professor, at George Washington University."

"I used to be a professor myself, in my early days, before I got into politics. Political Science. It all seemed a little phoney to me, standing in front of a class when I hadn't *done* anything. Which is why I got into politics for real. And I've never regretted it, Klein, not for a moment. Though every once in a while I look back to that academic life, and wonder if it wasn't so bad." Sansone shook his head. "Politics is a killing business. But there's nothing like it."

"Actually, I've practiced some law."

"Teaching is a noble profession, perhaps the most noble, Klein. After all, what's more important than the next generation? Your students must be an enormous satisfaction to you, when you see them leaving your classroom and entering life and going on to be a success in whatever field they may choose."

Was this the kind of bullshit Sansone served up to academics to get their votes? Klein asked himself.

"There's probably no deeper satisfaction," Sansone continued, "than passing on your experience to the next generation; it's the closest thing we have to immortality."

"I'm not very religious myself," Klein confessed, and then immediately regretted it. Had he said something unpolitical? But who was really religious these days? "I mean," he went on, "I've never exactly believed in someone up there who controls events, though I've got values."

"Yes, of course. You'll excuse me, Klein, just a moment. There's a person I have to talk to. Smith. He'll be our man, you'll remember, for European affairs. Yes, J. Zachariah Smith."

"It's been nice . . ."

"Do you know the man with him, Morris Friedlander?"

"Of course. Well, I don't actually *know* him."

"They just appointed him. He'll play the President's Special Assistant for Foreign Affairs. Too bad Mitch Murray couldn't make it tonight. I heard Evie's been sick." Sansone held up his glass, found it empty, and instead of going over to talk to Smith, he lurched toward the drinks table.

■ **Each team division will have its own Control color: White House, purple; State, blue; Defense, black; CIA, white; Treasury, red; and U.S. Information Agency, yellow.**

As he stood talking to Friedlander, Smith remembered that he'd slipped some on the social register. But Friedlander was still one of Washington's eligibles, creating an aura about himself for use in the next two or three decades in which he could look for a change of fortune. Meanwhile, here he was, the so-called brilliant young professor who had personified the intellectual side of Mitchell

Murray's campaign for those people, Smith thought, who were dazzled by pretension and had lost their faith in common sense. Did Friedlander really screw, Smith wanted to know, or was he simply another Hugh Hefner in a higher circle of deceit? It mattered who did it and who didn't. Smith trusted Southern senators, for all he hated them. They made it, they were the real thing, where the Friedlanders of the world gave you images, not anything you could count on.

"The issue, as I see it," Morris Friedlander was saying, "is to stabilize the area without a massive commitment. Simple, but not too simple. In the post-Vietnam era, if it ever comes, we must avoid such commitments. The lion must lie down with the lambs, coo with the doves."

"Morris, do you want to explain that?" Smith asked. "I thought there were quite a few lions in the region. Isn't that our problem?"

"Quite so. And, of course, we haven't even mentioned our friends, the Soviets."

"You mean Iran?"

"Control has created a little diversion for us there, which even further complicates the game. The role for the diplomatist will be a delicate one, but challenging, I should think."

"I guess I'm looking forward to it," Smith said. "We haven't been much in touch, but—you probably know—I was dumped six months ago as Assistant Secretary for Europe, and put in charge of Career Development. It's been pretty slow. Well, how do *you* find running the foundation?"

"Interesting, in an abstract sort of way. There's another job I might have preferred."

"I bet."

"I could have done worse, Zach. Losing an election throws one rather precipitously on the market."

"Yeah." There was Sally hovering nearby; he would have to introduce her. "Morris, have you met my wife? Sally, come over here, will you? Sally Jenks, this is Morris Friedlander."

Now he would have to stand watching Friedlander work her over. Didn't everyone get a catch in his throat, as he did, when he first saw her? God, she was beautiful, and vulnerable. Everyone must see that, too.

Could people see into *him* like that?

"Sally, in the game, Morris is the President's Special Assistant for Foreign Affairs."

She shouldn't wear a dress like this, not here, not in the Charles Francis Adams room, for Christ sake!

"Zach is all worked up about this game, so I know you must be, too," Sally said.

"Yes, rather. It should be amusing." Friedlander shot Sally a salacious look.

"I don't know exactly why anyone would want to play anything harder than checkers. I'm a great checkers player myself, but if I played anything more than that, I'd sure as hell want someone to pay me for it."

"We're being paid for it, Sally," Zach said.

"So then it's not really a game."

"People get paid for playing tennis and football."

"Those are work, honey. I once had a football player who was a close friend, and believe me, that's work. He used to come home after every game all banged up, and he'd just sit around the house groaning for days."

"I suspect," Friedlander said with a leer, "we'll be doing a bit of groaning ourselves before too many days have passed."

Friedlander finally left, and Smith found himself alone with Sally in the middle of the parquet floor.

"Zach, let's go outside on the balcony for a minute, and look at the lights. Would you like to?"

"Sure, I guess."

"It's the first week in December, and yet it's not cold at all."

"Winters aren't so bad in Washington," Zach said. "There aren't real winters here, like everything else in this city, just kind of nothing winters."

"This is about as far north as I ever got, though when I was a little girl, Zach, I used to dream about being the Snow Queen—that was my favorite book, it was almost my only book. So you could say that I *did* have winters, well, winters like those little glass bulbs you turn upside down and everything begins to snow inside. I mean, it was all in my mind, do you see?"

"Okay."

"It's beautiful out here. Aren't you glad we came?"

"I guess I am."

"There's the Watergate, and there's the Kennedy Center, and there's the Pentagon, and on your left, ladies and gentlemen . . . Honey, do you think there's someone looking at us, and asking if we see it as beautiful as He does?"

Zach said, "If you're talking about the same person I think you're talking about, I'd guess He wouldn't think we were very beautiful, or anything we did."

"I know you're thinking of all the little deals going on, and all the . . . well, that people are bad inside, but that's why it's different at night, and when you look at it from so far away, it *is* different. Now do you see why I wanted to come out here?"

"I said I did."

"You're a little grouchy tonight, Zach."

"I'm sorry, honey. Tomorrow I'll feel different." He looked out over the lights of the city. "The game, it's just so elaborate, that's all. I know I'm getting paid for it, and it's supposed to be useful, but still, I wish it were one thing or another."

"Are you sorry you're doing it?"

"No, I signed up for it."

"All right then. Can you kiss me here without getting all embarrassed if someone sees us?"

"Oh, they'd just think it was quaint."

"Do you *want* to kiss me?"

"Yes."

■ Operations will be conducted in real time. Standard
military time will be observed. When it is 2300 hours
in Washington, it is 0400 hours the next day in
London, 0600 in Moscow, 1100 in Bangkok and noon
in Peking (see chart). The problem begins one year
from now, on December 7.

To Frank Sansone, Stoddard Holmes looked frail and incon-
sequential. Why should Sansone bother with him, except, as the
game's Assistant Secretary for Far Eastern Affairs, Holmes represented a bureau whose support he'd need.

"A bit premature," Holmes said, in response to Sansone's pitch
for a strong UN role. "Perhaps we should wait for the realities of the
day."

Holmes didn't have a constituency in life. Who would vote for
him, that elegant stick?

"Well," Sansone persisted, "if we're going to settle things in that
part of the world, it seems to me that the UN is the best agency to do
the job."

"Perhaps. But there are often realities in such matters beyond
what might loosely be termed pretense and show. Put in all candor to
you, Senator, the UN will be your concern. I state it from the outset."

"I appreciate that."

"That's not to say," Holmes went on, "that the World
Organization might not prove of value. It is just to express a bit of
skepticism about what might be called a UN solution."

"It's usually horseshit."

"Quite so."

"I think I know horseshit when I smell it," Sansone said.

"I imagine you would."

"I was a delegate in New York not so many years ago."

"With your experience there, you will no doubt be adept at
seeing the possibilities, as well as the limitations."

"I'm looking forward to the next few weeks, aren't you?" Samsone asked.

"Indeed. And as I contemplate the rigors to which I imagine we will all be subjected, I come to the not-too-startling conclusion, Senator, that perhaps it's my bedtime, and that my wife and I should take our leave." Holmes gave an ironic smile. "A person you just might find useful is Michael Klein. An alliance between the UN Bureau and the Legal Advisory Office is not uncommon, in my experience. Have you spoken with him?"

"I did, and he seemed interested."

"I imagine he would be, though we only briefly chatted this afternoon." Holmes extended his thin hand. "Well, you will excuse me."

Senator Frank R. Sansone, the designated Assistant Secretary of State for International Organization Affairs, slipped into his paisley pajamas. Well, the UN wasn't much, but it was all Control had given him. But if it was only a game, why was he so anxious? His heart felt like an alarm clock.

■ **Players are responsible for assigning priorities to all communications received.**

By the time they were home, Sally Jenks had put everything else out of his mind. J. Zachariah Smith, the Assistant Secretary of State for European Affairs, wanted to make love. Every surface was soft, and then miraculously hard, and then soft again. Sally struggled and cried and tossed under him, Jesus Christ, heading down the bomb-run; but when he was on target, he dropped everything he had. For just an instant he saw Sally turn away like a desecrated landscape.

There was nothing, nothing left. He looked about after his plane had gone down, the stars twinkling over the wheat land northeast of Kiev.

> ■ **Players may communicate with members of their own team in any way they choose. Records of communications need not be maintained.**

His heart would explode with its gears and pins all over the floor. Like hell! Frank Sansone, the Assistant Secretary for International Organization Affairs, sucked in his breath.

"Frank, I'm making myself a nightcap. Want one?" Anne asked.

"Whatever it is they served me an hour ago has already worn off. Yeah, I'd like a Scotch."

Anne stood with the bathroom light behind her. Then he heard her going down the stairs. They still squeaked even after the carpenter had come. These Georgetown houses cost a mint and weren't worth a plugged nickel. Well, it had been closer to the action than suburbs like Bethesda or Chevy Chase. Now this house ate up every cent he had. And Gilda, his last, was going to college next year, so he'd have two there again, with the tuition getting worse and worse. How in the hell was he going to swing it? Where was that Scotch? If Anne hadn't found a job, and a goddamn good one, too, he'd be up the creek!

COMMUNIQUÉS IN THE NIGHT

WHITE: SATELLITE OBSERVATION READOUT CENTER, DEC 2, 1332 HRS, FLASH IMMEDIATE (PASS TO PRESIDENT)

TOP SECRET

LAUNCH SITES MAINLAND CHINA HAVE NOW REACHED STAGE COMPLETION.

Sally Jenks was going to sleep now, her body becoming heavy, a little cool. All her cognitive machinery had long since been put into her body, so that when it slept, her mind would have to crawl out again like a drunk who had fallen into a ditch. She slept as if the map of the world had been erased.

Zach Smith could wake up his wife and do it again; he'd probably be able to now. The engines of his plane were warming up on the airfield before the first light had broken, the air heavy with dampness, lights here and there still spreading, contracting. Northeast of Kiev, he would suddenly find himself—it was always the same place—

light, almost weightless. It was after the Bomb. *He* had dropped it, but nothing had happened!

☆ ☆ ☆

BLACK: BATTLEFIELD SUMMARY, COMMANDER, US FORCES VIET NAM, DEC 2, 1600 HRS

SECRET

CHICOM FORCE DIVISIONAL STRENGTH ENGAGED US UNITS IN SHARP EXCHANGE SOUTH OF HANOI AS US CONTINUED ADVANCE ALONG WIDE FRONT. B52S, BASED UDON THANI, THAILAND, STAGED MASSIVE RAIDS CHICOM BORDER.

☆ ☆ ☆

Well, it could happen, Smith thought. Who could count on our restraint? Or on theirs?

Did the Chinese need the provocation we seemed to be supplying them?

There had been no scenario, except to say it was a year in the future. He'd put all the game material in his in-box, on the left side; the real stuff—the material for the Career Development Office—on the right. Weren't these games supposed to give you a scenario? Weren't you supposed to know where you stood when the problem started?

They'd given him a pile of papers, telegrams, staff studies, intelligence reports. But wasn't that the way it always worked? And then you pieced it together?

And you said, This is it.

Except then, things would come unstuck. You thought you had it, and then some son-of-a-bitch got shot, or some general did a damn fool thing, or some defense you had counted on collapsed.

And you had to start up again with an entirely different situation, not that different, but different enough, so that all the balances would be changed, and what might have worked just the day before would no longer apply.

You never crossed the same *real* river twice. And yet you played games, because you thought you might cross that river some day. Well, he'd play. It hardly mattered if he were away from his regular job in Career Development. He'd put off the few appointments he'd scheduled, holding hands with has-been senior officers, men like himself who had somehow slipped from power, and were casting about. Fitch could handle the semiannual report. He'd play the game. It must be better than Career Development.

Once he'd been a piece of that running set of gears, springs, and pins, with nodes at Washington, London, Moscow, flashing metallic yellows, reds, and blues. Once he'd been an Assistant Secretary of State in the intricate stress of all that machinery. To be part of it was all he'd ever hoped for. Was that true? And if it was true, why had he slipped, why had he blown up in front of the Soviet Ambassador, "embarrassed the Service," as they'd put it, so that they had dropped him back to this sandlot job, a living, visible failure?

They had been his friends, but as soon as he was in trouble, *they* had kicked him out, *they* had refused to reconsider. The Under Secretary had disclaimed any responsibility. "If it were my decision, Zach, you know how things would have gone." He hadn't had the guts to ask whose decision it was.

Had he done it to himself, as Dr. Marvin had diffidently suggested? Or had they also found out about Sally's past . . . or his?

Why hadn't Sally put him to sleep? He was okay now. He didn't have to be haunted by this fear, as he had all these years, that it would come out, that somehow they would finally see the records, and . . . He could take a pill. He would soon, but not yet.

Blue: American Embassy Warsaw, November 30

SECRET

Verbatim of the 152ⁿᵈ Ambassadorial Talk between the United States and the People's Republic of China

Ambassador Woo: The note of the People's Republic of China, dated November 27, expresses its position exactly. The failure of your government to accept the note is the clearest indication of the truth of the points raised therein. The United States is clearly interested in attacking the People's Republic of China, but it is unwilling that its shameful motives be unmasked. Rather, it resorts to the pretext of rejecting the note of the People's Republic of China on non-substantive grounds. The peoples of the world will not be taken in by such clumsy attempts at deception. The invasion plans of the ruling militaristic clique of the United States and its stooges will be shown for what they are.

Ambassador Peters: I do not feel that any purpose is served by indulging in invectives or in wild flights of imagination. I therefore will ask bluntly whether or not your government is prepared to begin discussions of the substantive issues raised in your note of November 27?

Ambassador Woo: Then your government accepts the note?

Ambassador Peters: No, the note was rejected and returned to your Embassy.

Ambassador Woo: Then I will return to our original topic, the military occupation by the United States of the territory of the People's Republic of China, specifically, Formosa, the Pescadores, and the offshore islands, as listed in our aide-memoire of March 3. Following that, I will raise a second topic, the military occupation by the United States of the People's Republic of Viet Nam. Following that, I will raise a third topic, the military occupation of the Republic of Laos and the Kingdom of Cambodia. Following that, I will raise . . .

Ambassador Peters: Mr. Ambassador, I can see no purpose in this tedious recital.

☆ ☆ ☆

Sally's body moved like a land mass against his, the drift of a continent. Smoke rose now over Hamburg, Lübeck next, raked by flak. So peaceful up there, the puffs of flak opening up like sea anemone, any piece of which could tear his plane to shreds. The steady drone of his plane; the tight press of his gear; the fixed spatial relations of the crew, while outside the fighters beat off the Focke-wulfs and Messerschmidts. A steel tube would penetrate his body, burn away his penis.

Smoke rose now from the plane as it passed over Lübeck.

Zach had thought of women, or tried to, only to return to that awful scene at Lorton Academy when the Captain had torn away the blankets. He and Gary hadn't done anything, at least not yet, but he would have; he would have gone ahead and done it just because he was too panicked not to. Maybe he should have tried. Maybe that would have settled it, that he wasn't really interested? The Captain had hushed it up, hadn't wanted it out that *that* sort of thing went on at Lorton. And then, for the next five years, when he'd wanted to leave, the Captain had held it over him.

Zach had lived through it. You lived through anything, sitting in a bomber trying to imagine sexy women, wondering whether you might feel more in your cock than in your stomach, as your plane drifted slowly over Europe on its way back to England.

White: Satellite Observation Read-Out Center, December 6
(Pass to President)

TOP SECRET

Test monitoring of Chinese missiles clearly indicates that they now pose the possibility of reaching mainland United States.

Given the speed at which the Chinese launching capability has progressed, and the many technical problems incident to concealment, the figure of eight-five payloads represents a fairly reliable estimate.

Such missiles now radically alter the strategic situation in Far East, and could change our options in the present conflict. The Chinese missile sites, however, are extremely vulnerable to conventional as well as nuclear attack.

Stoddard Holmes asked himself, what if he'd been standing on his head when, say, an ambassador had come in—well, Ney, for instance? "Cable Bangkok! ASSISTANT SECRETARY OF STATE FAR EASTERN AFFAIRS IS MAD, NO RPT NO INSANE. WIRE INSTRUCTIONS."

"But my dear fellow," Holmes said, putting himself right-side-up. "You yourself said the problem needed looking at from an entirely different angle."

"So I did, so I did," said the Thai Ambassador, with a Shakespearean jollity about him which the sly little bastard certainly never had.

"So good to see you, Ney," Holmes said, hand outstretched. Ney is what they had called him at Cambridge, he'd confessed upon their second meeting, and Holmes had made a note to remember.

"I'm so glad at this moment to have the opportunity . . ." A trace of Mozart flitted in.

"I needn't say," Holmes went on, "that your concern is fully shared not only in this office but throughout the Department, indeed, by the President himself, who, I am informed, at this very moment is composing a suitable response." Why was it, Stoddard asked himself, now fully awake as he nestled under the covers, that he'd always taken such an Edwardian tone with people like Ney?

BLUE: AMERICAN CONSUL GENERAL HONG KONG, DEC
3, 1140 HRS

SECRET

   BRITISH GOV, SIR ERIC PERTH, PASSED ME HIS
SUMMARY INDICATIONS COMPILED LAST FEW WEEKS
THAT RED SHIELD LEADERSHIP HAS QTE BURNT ITS
BRIDGES UNQTE AND WILL USE FORCE ALONG EVER
WIDENING FRONT.

                                    MCGUIRE

☆ ☆ ☆

Ney stood out in his mind like a cloisonné jar on an illumined
shelf. As the light faded, the metal strips between the porcelain
crackled and glowed with static electricity. Why, Holmes asked
himself, had he chosen to spend his life with people like Ney, who
weighed so little?

   A raw-boned giant of a man, half a head taller than himself, his
father advanced over clods of earth, holding two Thais by their
collars. They dangled like watch-fobs; they jerked like the dead.

   Cross-legged by the porcelain stove, his father would have
enjoyed a *têté-à-têté* with the pygmy peoples, their sly priapic
approaches, their elliptical orbiting of issues. His eyes twinkled, and
the small lines around them cracked.

   Holmes felt callused hands on his chest and back as his father,
the town doctor of Elton, examined him on a summer's day over
sixty years ago, with his fine-grained sense of organic conspiracy.
Holmes's body was weak, his bones like a chicken's. It wouldn't take
much. The air in his home was quiet with expectation, as if from the
first day of his life it had patiently waited.

   "Big man now," his father had said, with neither envy nor
disinterest. The town was a little proud, perhaps, of having produced

30

a U.S. ambassador. Now it waited for him to return to Elton and die there, to be like his father before *his* death, gossiping maliciously with the neighbors, puttering about in his garden, playing the philosopher.

☆ ☆ ☆

BLUE: AMEMBASSY BANGKOK, DEC 3, 1530 HRS (PASS TO PRESIDENT)

TOP SECRET

IN VIEW INCREASING THREATS BY NEW CHICOM LEADERSHIP, I ASSURED PREMIER WE WLD STAND BY TREATY OBLIGATIONS.

AT HIS INSISTENCE, I AGREED INQUIRE DEPT IF APPROPRIATE HIGH LEVEL STATEMENT, PREFERABLY BY PRESIDENT, MIGHT BE MADE TO LEND THAIS FURTHER ASSURANCE. PREMIER SAID HE APPRECIATED MY EFFORTS AND HOPED STATEMENT WLD BE FORTHCOMING. PREMIER SAID EVEN MORE IMPORTANT WLD BE OUR DISPATCH OF ADDITIONAL MILITARY UNITS. IN CANDID ASIDE, HE ADDED MORALE THAI UNITS IN NORTH EXTREMELY LOW, AND THEIR ABILITY RESIST ANY CHINESE INVASION QUITE LIMITED.

STRACHEY

☆ ☆ ☆

Holmes slipped farther down into the cold sheets while Betty slept like a turned-off TV set. Had his father been faithful, or had his passion for small-town gossip been sufficient compensation? Was Ney faithful, with his pillow of a high-caste wife, with her sleepy-winking eyes? Probably not. Representations in a Bond Street suit, but in bed, he probably wore a headband and a silk robe.

Each member of the delegation is authorized to purchase one blue suit. "Blue," mind you, their position book photostated by the CIA, and deposited on his desk—such a delectable tidbit, bless them! Of course, it had no intelligence value, but the "one blue suit" *was* a compensation. Without such moments, how could he have endured it all these years?

☆ ☆ ☆

White: Field Operative 547, American Consulate Tabriz, November 30

TOP SECRET

In recent weeks, there has been a substantial flow of clandestine operatives from the Soviet Union into Northern Iran. It is believed that these operatives have been trained at a secret KGB base in Baku.

Soviet equipment is also passing into the hands of the rebel tribesmen. Large numbers of rifles and automatic weapons have already arrived. Several usually reliable sources indicate that the Soviets have promised the rebels T-55 tanks and artillery.

☆ ☆ ☆

Frank Sansone placed the drink on the edge of the tub, then eased his huge body into the water. Who was it, that Under Secretary of Defense he'd read about in the *Post*, who'd sat in his office at the Pentagon drinking cups of hot water trying to keep awake—then was found dead in the middle of the night by a cleaning woman? He reached for his drink. "Anne, this bathtub Scotch is great!" She came in and wiped the sweat off his forehead with a cold cloth, then did his back.

"Do you know what I'm going to do tomorrow in the game? I've got it all figured out. I'm asking for a conference—it'll be at the UN—

to get this whole mess in the Far East right out on the table."

"Sounds good, Frank."

"I'll get that conference, too. 'Course, the important thing is to make it *mean* something, really use it to settle things in that part of the world."

"I suppose that's the idea of the game, but, my God, Frank, the UN? Remember what you thought of it, when you did your stint up there?"

"Yeah, I wanted to break every window in that building." He laughed. "Anne, you wouldn't believe the way those people sit around on their multicolored asses."

"Now it's your baby, so you got to love it, right, honey?"

"That's what they're paying me for."

"It can't be any worse than a buyers' conference."

She was tired, too. She was working too hard, but now that he had a job, he was bringing in the money again.

" Now, all I got to worry about is the European and Asian desks, that's Zach Smith and Stoddard Holmes. I made a straight pitch to Holmes for a strong UN role, but I think he hates the UN as much as I do."

"Oh, I remember him at the party," Anne said. "The one with little cracks around his eyes?"

"Yeah, that's him. Stoddard Holmes. He was a fixture at State for years. Every so often they'd dust him off and send him out to some godforsaken place with a tin roof and the rain leaking through. I know, because we had to confirm him." Sansone shook his head. "Well, he probably won't be any help."

"Want another drink?"

"Sure. You know, Anne, this game, I don't know why the hell I let myself get involved in it. I'm already working my ass off, and it hasn't even started. Forget the drink. Let's go to bed!"

He slid in under the covers. The moon caught the sheet so that it shimmered like a glacier or a sail, and he slept.

☆ ☆ ☆

BLUE: AMEMBASSY BANGKOK, DEC 4, 1253 HRS (PASS TO PRESIDENT)

TOP SECRET

PREMIER TULALAMBA CALLED ME IN TO SHOW NOTE JUST DELIVERED BY CHICOM AMBASSADOR I CHENG LOH. PREMIER REPORTS HE TOLD AMBASSADOR NOTE WLD RECEIVE SERIOUS STUDY BUT SUCH PHRASES AS QTE CRIMINAL COMPLICITY UNQUOTE AND QTE SQUATTING HOLE FOR AMERICAN MILITARISTS UNQUTE EXCEEDED BOUNDS DIPLOMATIC PARLANCE.

PREMIER HAD GONE ON DISCUSS SUBSTANCE NOTE TELLING AMBASSADOR THAT US MILITARY INSIDE THAILAND WAS ENTIRELY THAI AFFAIR, BUT THAT IT CONSTITUTED NO THREAT TO PEOPLE'S REPUBLIC. RATHER CHINESE TROOPS IN DIVISIONAL STRENGTH ON LAO BORDER CONSTITUTED SERIOUS THREAT TO THAILAND.

FOR YOUR INFORMATION ONLY: IF THAIS ARE TO STAND UP TO CHICOMS, THEY WILL NEED BOTH MORAL AND EXTENSIVE ADDITIONAL MILITARY SUPPORT. PLEASE ADVISE.

STRACHEY

Michael Klein read to his wife from de Callières on the art of the diplomatist. *"He should pay attention to women, but never lose his heart. He must be able to simulate dignity even if he does not possess it."* Then he asked with a perversity which even he wondered at, "What do you think de Callières means by dignity?"

He'd put the question to his class in International Law just last week. But now, as he asked Catherine, he braced himself as if he were about to have alcohol splashed on a cut.

"You remember," she answered, "that quip of J.P. Morgan? 'If you have to ask what a yacht costs, you shouldn't own one.' "

"Do you think de Callières thinks dignity is something external or internal?"

"My God, you're pedantic!"

"I just thought you'd be interested in the question. Maybe I put it wrong, okay?"

"Mr. Humble. I'd rather see you angry. It's good for you."

"You're making a virtue of necessity—one, darling, you've pushed me to."

"Don't call me darling when you don't mean it. You always get unctuous when you're really angry. I'd rather you were just plain vicious and had it out."

"You've said that before."

"You don't seem to hear inside your tower, with its pigeons and bells and that rope hanging down between your teeth." Catherine barely got through the last word before she was crying, and then the crying took hold of her in hysterical spasms. Still another night they wouldn't make love.

BLUE: AMEMBASSY TEHERAN, DEC 5, 1400 HRS (PASS TO PRESIDENT)

TOP SECRET

PREMIER ANSARY TOLD ME INFUSION SOV ARMS AND TRAINED CADRES HAD COMPLETELY ALTERED STRATEGIC POSITION RE NORTHERN TRIBESMEN AT TIME IRAN GOV IS LEAST ABLE TO COPE. SHAH REMAINS UNIMPROVED, AND EVEN SHOULD HE SURVIVE ASSASSINATION ATTEMPT, HE IS NOT LIKELY TO BE EFFECTIVE FORCE SOME TIME.

PREMIER CONFESSES HE HAS NO POPULAR FOLLOWING AND LITTLE RESPECT FROM MAJOR FORCES COUNTRY, INCLUDING ARMY. IN HIS VIEW, WITHOUT STRONG US SUPPORT, IRAN MAY NOT PUT UP FIGHT, AND MAY SEEK COMPROMISE SOLUTION OF GRANTING SOME AUTONOMY TO NORTHERN PROVINCES.

ANSARY WOULD LIKE SEE US FORCE IN IRAN, PERHAPS 30,000 TROOPS, AS TOKEN OUR SUPPORT TO BOOST SAGGING IRANIAN MORAL. I INDICATED LITTLE LIKELIHOOD EFFORT OUR PART THIS MAGNITUDE, BUT PROMISED TRANSMIT MESSAGE.

CUMMINGS

Klein watched his wife go into the bathroom and close the door. Catherine would stand now in front of the mirror, as if restoring an old masterpiece. She could never clean her face enough, so that she would go to bed still somewhat repulsive to herself. Her teeth were yet another ritual of cleaning, gargling, and spitting.

"Aren't you through yet?"

"You can go to sleep," Catherine answered.

"I'd like to wait for you."

"I don't want to make love tonight. I'm still too tense."

She started to undress. "Don't wear anything," Klein said. Her figure was still stunning. Having Helen had rounded out her hips and only made them more desirable. He should have liked to call her from the office and rush home to make love; it was a fantasy she'd always managed to defeat. Now he moved his body over hers, and kissed her, and even as she pulled away, he felt the pleasure of his own physical longing. When that became uncomfortable, he lay back.

"Did I tell you? The Chinese Communists are supposed to have long-range nuclear missiles, about eighty-five, to be exact. I just saw the CIA report, which was classified Top Secret. If it were the real thing, of course, I wouldn't be able to discuss it with you."

"But what if it wasn't a game after all? We'd all be in serious danger, Michael."

He said nothing.

"How about Senator Sansone's idea for a UN session?"

Again—was it sheer perversity?—he said nothing.

"Frankly," Catherine went on, "I doubt the United Nations could do anything. We've never agreed on that. You can talk and talk, but ultimately countries do what they want. They're vicious, just like people."

"That's probably true," he finally said, "though I still think that analogies from people to governments can be dangerous. I only said the UN could be useful sometimes."

He was tired enough. "Kiss me," he said. He turned away and went to sleep.

☆ ☆ ☆

BLUE: AMEMBASSY MOSCOW, DEC 4, 1220 HRS (PASS TO PRESIDENT)

TOP SECRET

THIS MORNING I ATTEMPTED DISCUSS WORSENING SITUATION SE ASIA WITH DEPUTY FOREIGN MINISTER BUKOVSKY IN VIEW KUZNETSOV'S SECRET MISSION TO PEKING. SOVS HAVE STILL MADE NO RPT NO PUBLIC ANNOUNCEMENT OF KUZNETSOV'S VISIT SO THAT OUR KNOWLEDGE THIS EVENT SHOULD STILL BE TIGHTLY HELD.

TO MY QUESTION OF HOW SOVS ASSESSED CHINESE INTENTIONS RE THAILAND, BUKOVSKY SAID SOVS WERE NOT THEIR DIPLOMATIC REPRESENTATIVES, AS US WELL KNEW. SOVS WOULD REGRET ANY EXPANSION OF WAR

THO THEY WOULD NOT BE UNSYMPATHETIC IN VIEW
QTE CONTINUAL US PROVOCATIONS UNQTE. HOW DID
SOVS ASSESS FUTURE IN SE ASIA? BUKOVSKY SAID HE
COULD NOT SPECULATE.

WHEN I RAISED QUESTION OF IRAN, HE REPLIED MY
ALLEGATION SOVS HAVE MOVED OPERATIVES INTO AREA
IS QTE A COMPLETE FABRICATION UNQTE.

ROLAND

Sally Jenks slept heavily, resisting Zach Smith's efforts to wake her up. He caressed her, sucked her breasts, making her nipples hard and erect. "Oh, you son-of-a-bitch. You beautiful, greedy bastard. Leave me alone. Can't you see what I want? Stop it. Sleepy, let me sleep." Her hands were on him. "Here, come here, come here." She took it, and moved it up and down her open lips. "Oh Zach, I like it." She sucked it, turned her tongue around it. His fingers were in her, moving up and down, and then he was like a missile rising from its pad, then higher and higher, and exploding into the sky, as she clawed the skin on his back.

"Are you up *now*?" he asked her.

"Sure am, honey." Sally sat up in bed. "Did you get any sleep?"

"I did for a few minutes. I was flying over Germany again, and then I woke up, and started thinking about you." He sat up and faced her. "Did you like the get-together last night?"

"It was all right. I didn't mind. I still, even after—how long have we been together?—I still feel over my head."

"Sally, you're doing fine."

"I remember, Zach, when I used to work the Hill. I'd go to parties like this with congressmen and senators, all sorts of important people. But I always felt it right in my stomach. I'd say, 'Here we go, Sally Jenks,' and then I'd walk in with those faces staring at me. They knew, they always knew what I was doing there." She gave a little laugh. "You got to be good at *something*. It's, as you say, my special area of competence. And now that I'm middle-aged . . . Are you listening to me, Zach?"

"Uh-huh. You were wonderful. I'm lucky. I was fifty-two when I married you. I never thought it would happen."

"Sometimes, Zach, you're not really here. I mean like right now, and even when we make love, you're sort of, what do you call it, on automatic pilot? Do you know what I mean?"

"Yes."

"It *was* good, Zach."

"I guess I felt funny tonight. Things started coming together again, like when I blew up at the Soviet Ambassador and I had that breakdown, or whatever they called it. When you're the Assistant Secretary, even if it's not real like now, you no longer feel you're living *through* a crisis; you feel you *are* the crisis."

Sally waited for him.

"Well, in this game . . . the Soviets are screwing us in Iran, and the Chinese have troops massed near Thailand, and they're supposed to be meeting together in Peking. They're probably making a deal, like they did with the Hitler-Stalin Pact. And then it's all going to blow up. It looks bad."

"Zach, you're all worked up. It's just a game."

He stands by the railing of a ship to Leningrad. He has so much to do—how will he get it all done! He clutches at the papers in his breast pocket: his passport, visa, his instructions, his marriage certificate.

The ship, still at some speed, bears down onto the dock. Then it stops, with a rush of people funneling through the open end.

"Have you evidence for your diplomatic immunity? Submit, Mr. Smith."

"Of course, I have . . ."

"Check for venereal disease."

"This is ridiculous. I submit only under protest."

"X-ray records."

"How can you expect the United States and the Soviet Union to have a fruitful diplomatic exchange, which is certainly *our* intention, gentlemen, if you treat me . . ."

"Submit, Mr. Smith."

"Athletic supporter, medium or small?"

"I refuse to fill this out."

"Psychiatric report."

"I don't have a psychiatrist."

"Dr. Marvin has been so good as to submit . . . records which make your condition unmistakably clear."

Stoddard Holmes meets with the Chinese Ambassador in a house of prostitution in Bangkok. The Ambassador wears a mandarin collar and sits stiffly in a wicker chair with a dragon-carved back.

Young boys with flowering penises, as well as almost hairless girls, frisk about. Holmes, dressed in a white suit, occasionally touches and strokes the adolescents of both sexes. "If you could only enter into the spirit of things," he says, sipping an iced drink. "I'm sure we could reach agreement, at least *en principe.*"

"No doubt," says the Chinese Ambassador, and makes a sudden rush at Holmes, who scurries away to find himself in the marshes near Elton. There, pulled up in the mud, is a rowboat without oars.

For a moment, he found himself wide awake. But what, after all, did Betty expect of him? It was such a tedious business, and yet he'd hired her, or married her, for business equally tedious. He slept again. In the morning, if he remembered, he'd marvel at such moments of lucidity. It was like meeting himself coming around a corner. He'd imagine many Stoddard Holmeses, now here, now there, all the same, epiphanies of himself, spying on one another, catching one another in hurried yet rewarding glances.

☆ ☆ ☆

BLACK: COMMANDER, US FORCES THAILAND, DEC 4,
1220 HRS, FLASH IMMEDIATE (PASS TO PRESIDENT)

TOP SECRET

CHINESE FORCES NOW EXCEED 375,000. MAJOR
ELEMENTS HAVE CROSSED MEKONG INTO WESTERN
LAOS AND ARE HEADING SOUTH TO THREATENING
POSITION ON THAI BORDER.

☆ ☆ ☆

When Frank Sansone arrives at the first meeting, there is the Secretary of State, rat face, squinting little eyes, a scar that puts a line through his right eyebrow. It's the boss, Nick D'Antonio!

"You was always a little wet behind the ears, kid, but you looked good in those days," D'Antonio says. "You made us all look good, and that's the point, ain't it?"

But over D'Antonio's voice is that of Mansefield Vane. "Unpleasant as it may sound to your *amour propre*, I must point out, Senator, that your proposal looks rather shoddy. Your staff work, to say the least, leaves something to be desired." Holmes, Smith, even Michael Klein, who wears a rabbinic hat, laugh at the miserable sheaf of crumpled papers Sansone has presented.

"You're a big boy now," D'Antonio goes on. "I can't promise you that seat in Congress, but I'll make damn sure you get it."

"You've ignored the most obvious fact of the case," Vane says. "Thailand is in Africa." Everyone nods.

D'Antonio says, "You're a big boy now, Franco. I'll do what I can, but frankly, you're gettin' to be trouble."

"But Thailand's in Asia," Sansone protests. Vane, everyone, laughs at his obvious mistake.

41

BLACK: COMMANDER, US FORCES THAILAND, DEC 7, 1520 HRS (PASS TO PRESIDENT)

TOP SECRET

REGULAR CHICOM UNITS REPORTED PREVIOUS TELS MASSED WEST SIDE MEKONG. SHOULD SUCH UNITS CROSS FROM LAO STAGING AREA, THEY WLD NO DOUBT SEEK LINK WITH COMMUNIST REBELS IN MOUNTAINS TO CONSOLIDATE NORTHERN THAILAND.

WE ARE MAINTAINING FULL AERIAL RECONNAISSANCE. WHILE MANEUVERS MAY BE MERE ADDITIONAL THREAT ON THAI GOV, WE BELIEVE THIS MAY BE THE REAL THING.

☆ ☆ ☆

As Klein walks by, a man who looks like J.P. Morgan sticks out the crook of his cane. Klein trips, and then begs Morgan's pardon in a way which should have drawn an immediate apology, but none comes. Each time he attempts to walk away, there is Morgan's cane. He can see himself being tripped in multiple pictures, as if in a kaleidoscope.

"There's clearly no legal solution," Klein says. "We're dealing here with a question of force."

Morgan waits with a sneer. It certainly *is* a question of force. What is Klein going to do about it?

"Leave," he says.

"Try it," Morgan answers. "Besides, you've a daughter." Morgan raises his cane as if to strike him.

"You're not thinking," Klein says.

"No," answers Morgan, and as he puts down his stick, Klein

suddenly begins to beat his head and body. Klein's fists bleed, lose pieces of flesh.

BLACK: COMMANDER, US FORCES THAILAND, DEC 7, 1625 HRS, FLASH IMMEDIATE (PASS TO PRESIDENT)

TOP SECRET

UNITS 12TH AND 23RD CHINESE ROUTE ARMIES HAVE CROSSED MEKONG INTO THAILAND.

At 4:25 a.m., Washington time, Frank Sansone, the Assistant Secretary of State for International Organization Affairs, is dreaming that he is being investigated for election fraud. The Legal Advisor, Michael Klein, and the Assistant Secretary of State for European Affairs, J. Zachariah Smith, are in deep sleep, with long, slow brain waves. At the same moment, Stoddard Holmes, the Assistant Secretary of State for Far Eastern Affairs, dreams that the Chinese Communists have gathered in a great arc with drawn spears, and that, at a signal, they have converged into the circle of one suspended truck tire.

THE FIRST DAY

Zach Smith reached for the phone. It was 5:07. He asked a few questions in a subordinating tone to the Control officer, and was on his feet. He had to hand it to them. They were playing the game completely straight! 5:07!

Sally Jenks lay on her side, her breasts vagrant. As Zach scrambled, she slowly became dishpan, drawn, and coordinated. She reached for her robe and cigarettes, then staggered toward the hall on her way to the kitchen to make coffee.

Morning would be breaking soon, the slow wave of light rolling back the gray like an atomic bomb in ultra-slow motion. He would be snapping and fumbling with his flight suit and gear as he ran out onto the airfield into the wave of light.

Frank Sansone lay unable to move. It was as if someone had been crouching behind a door and had suddenly yelled, Boo! The bastards, getting him up in the middle of the night. But he'd agreed to it; he was getting the money.

Anne was already out of bed, her robe on, her mouth tight as when she had something unpleasant to do. She did it well. She was so much quicker in the morning than he was. Why couldn't she pinch-hit for him in the game; well, why not?

He gulped down the coffee she'd made, and waited for facility to enter his mind. Before then, everything would have to be in slow motion, zipping his fly, tying his shoelaces, even kissing Anne.

He got into his car. It moved off, leaving Anne, already dressed for work, waving to him at the doorway. He was driving, and yet he was like a man crouching in a bomb shelter.

Michael Klein woke easily and, once he'd heard, he grinned to himself at the *elán* with which the game had started. Then he had the pleasure of scaring his wife with the news of the Chinese invasion and the threat of a nuclear exchange. She lay with her eyes open as if she'd fallen from a great height. Of course, he explained to her, it was just a game. But he'd been called. It meant he'd be in on the big decisions. Catherine did seem worried. Like a little girl, she believed in games. He hadn't time now to comfort her, though he made a few hurried gestures to indicate intent.

He went downstairs and fixed himself breakfast. He felt like Achilles taking a long lead on the tortoise. Were the Chinese actually invading Thailand? Would the United States be able to stop them? He'd want to pick up the mutual defense treaty with the Thais, the telegrams, protocols, the memoranda of conversation. Would the President order in additional units by simple Commander-in-Chief discretion? And beyond that? He'd already packed reprints of his journal article. A meeting at State, the National Security Council, and then, of course, his conference at the UN. It all fell neatly into place.

Blue: ARGOS Foundation Study, Department of State Contract
#17223B
"The Red Shield and the West," October 20

The Red Shield, which seized power in Mainland China last February, is hardly a tight organization by Leninist standards, or even by those of the western parliamentary world. It is essentially an alliance of young activists, with university and even secondary school students playing the leading roles. For organizations of comparable looseness and flexibility, one should look to certain radical American student groups. What has been surprising to Western observers is that this group has been able to seize power in a country where age and experience have traditionally ranked so high.

Although the Party machinery has been completely broken up, the Army and administrative bureaucracies are still generally intact, despite some changes at the top. In a sense, the Red Shield has been content to let older men administer its decrees. The effect has been that, while escaping responsibility itself, the Red Shield can blame their elders' "obstructionism" for any mistakes or shortcomings. Failure by the "black resisters" has meant public humiliations, beatings, and sometimes death.

What makes the Red Shield an unpredictable element are the extreme youth and inexperience of its leaders and their endorsement of "revolutionary enthusiasm," which some Western observers have called the "cult of the irrational."

Stoddard Holmes moved with cheerful deliberation. One might have expected Control, he thought, to have come up with a more subtle ploy than simply having the Chinese blunder into Thailand. Except that the new Chinese leadership, the Red Shield, was supposed to be made up of blunderers, "cultists of the irrational" in the briefing book, who made no sense at all, so apparently he shouldn't attempt to look for any.

But if one couldn't understand one's opponent, how could one play games with him, much less order the world? Hadn't that always been the trouble with Foggy Bottom, that it reduced its opponents to madmen, and so gave free run to its own paranoia?

Betty was already up, fixing his breakfast, laying out his coat, his Homburg, scarf, and umbrella.

But if one were in fact dealing with rational types, one could simply have divided up the world according to some factor of deliverable power—how else?—and be done with it. Southeast Asia, particularly now the Chinese had missiles, would then be *their* area. Why interfere? Holmes smiled.

No, it wouldn't work that way, at least for a while. We lacked the grace, he thought, to acquiesce in such inevitable logic. For every part of the world was always designated as *vital* to our interests. It always produced so much percentage of this metal (one he'd never heard of, which was supposed to be used in the turrets of jet engines), and so much of that; or if this country fell, another would fall, and then still another, and then, oh then, God help us, the very towers of Ilium would topple in some apocalyptic vision!

Holmes adjusted his Homburg, kissed Betty on the cheek—she had such trusting blue eyes; even squeezed her hand. "These are serious times, my dear." He headed briskly out the door to a waiting cab.

Sirens should have been blasting full force as Smith drove into the State Department, but instead it was a quiet, gliding ride in the early morning haze, like putting down in fog, the medic and firefighting trucks waiting on the airfield. The United States, Smith thought, had gotten nothing out of the Soviets, who'd probably know damn well what was going on, because they'd be in on the deal themselves.

He could see himself now with the Soviet Ambassador right there. He waited for his reaction, but nothing came. Smith shifted in his car seat. When he looked up, his mother was staring at the Ambassador with her overbearing stare: "I think, young man, you owe us all an explanation!" Smith smiled. He was crossing the District line; he would put it to the Soviets as soon as he could, no nonsense. But what if they'd be playing dumb because they *were* dumb? "When you don't know," his father'd told him, "it's probably the better part to say just that. Most people, even your mother, don't know everything." Father shuffled a bit in his tweedy hunting jacket. He usually managed to miss. Mother said, "If you don't know, say so!" She looked like the Queen of Hearts, and in a moment would have his head. What was it Smith hadn't known? As his car turned off Wisconsin Avenue, he drove with a sinking sense of failure and despair.

☆ ☆ ☆

The dream about the house of prostitution had raised certain questions in Holmes's mind, for at some point, hadn't a certain moral rigidity entered his character? No, moral rigidity wasn't the right term, but he would let that sit. His patronage of such places, at any rate, had ceased in his early thirties, and had been replaced by a somewhat compulsive if disengaged gregariousness.

He'd never actually fornicated with such women, but he'd enjoyed their youthful aesthetics of eye makeup and swishing silk, their tittering laughter, their awkward, still tender, movements. No, he'd only wanted a sip, a touch, the drollery of his expert Japanese; and they, the illusion of geisha class. They seemed to be dreaming, as if under a blanket of sleeping pills. Hadn't it been just a dream for him, one he'd protected by denying himself a final physical involvement?

No, moral rigidity was not the right term; it had been revulsion. On the highroads of Italy (his one assignment in the West), he'd found his confirmatory symbol. He could still see the women steaming like horses, their bellies swollen, their mouths like open wounds, waiting for the truckers, for the cart-drivers to take them off and spread their legs. He'd thought too much about them, a vice-consul in Naples with nothing to do but entertain visions of such squalor. They should erect monuments to them, like Henry Moore's statues, like conning towers, or stone temples—the Hiroshima Domes of the West!

Sansone's car eased down the Georgetown streets with their houses of clapboard and brick, self-conscious shutters, gas-lights, the old colonial fittings mere glazes on his mind. Underneath, a vision of the mafia boss, D'Antonio, seeped through. He would have to live with that image until he died. You never fought clear, you paid and paid, just as D'Antonio himself had made him pay twice over for every sin, and maybe then again. Triple bookkeeping.

Rat face, silk cravat, "Like the old days, Franco." Why couldn't D'Antonio leave him alone! He was finished now, out! "Leave me alone," Sansone cried aloud, writhing in his seat, then caught himself.

Had to think of the game. He'd wanted a meeting of the Security Council, but that was before the invasion—troops were in the field. What could the UN do now? "Inhibit our freedom of action," Professor Morgenstern had told him once in the darkened quiet of the Cosmos Club. *Realpolitik*, and from a Jew who'd gotten out of Auschwitz in an apple crate!

Just as his car tunneled through the Georgetown underpass, Sansone's mind snapped on. The UN action in Korea, he thought, that was the model. It had taken him a while, but now he had it. All they'd need would be a meeting or two to get it organized. And he'd control it, too. The UN under Sansone! Yes, he'd play the game, and he'd win. No shitting around! When Frank Sansone got into something, no matter what, he did it for keeps!

His coat over his arm, he strode into his assigned office. A secretary was already there, pouring him a cup of coffee.

"Good morning, Senator. Do you take cream and sugar?" He went into his office and shut the door. His eyes suddenly filled with tears. Months since he'd had a job, felt like a human being!

He came back out. The secretary—Martha, that was her name—was waiting, competent, attentive. "The briefing book is on your desk, Senator."

His aide, Wylie Adams, came in, but where were the others? The second man had called in sick. Sansone wanted all of them, the group of nine or ten, and sometimes more, he'd always had to listen to him. Where was McGrath, his speechwriter and long-time assistant? Why hadn't Control hired *him* like he'd asked? How could he work without McGrath? Wylie Adams seemed elegant and useless—pure State Department!

"Nice to see you up so early," Sansone said.

"It makes me feel neither healthy, wealthy, nor wise," Wylie Adams rejoined. "Merely sullen at Mother State for getting me into this mess, as if we didn't have messes enough for real. Five o'clock. It's obscene!"

"Adams, I want you to listen to what I've been thinking." Sansone saw Adans's face set and his smirk slowly fade. Where was McGrath?

As Klein went up the elevator shaft, he thought the crisis was an ideal opportunity to really do something, to be an agent, at least on paper, and not just a provider of legal advice. Lawyers, it didn't matter what kind, were so often just whores, selling their arguments to be used as *other* people saw fit. International law had seemed once to be above the usual pulling and grabbing. Except its lawyers, he'd found out too quickly, were used in just the same way: corrupted by policies other people had made, forced to pay lip service to meaningless phrases—a nation of law, world peace through world law.

His aides came in. Carolyn Carr, about thirty, had been only a year or two with the law firm of Phelps & Wyatt. "An attractive woman," he'd said to Catherine at last night's get-together as a way of neutralizing the fact he'd been staring at her. Catherine had responded that Carolyn Carr was probably good-looking, but only in a conventional way. Carolyn had been given the UN Legal Affairs job. Jay Wyzanski, a State Department lawyer, had been appointed his deputy.

Klein handed them reprints of his article in *International Law and Diplomacy*. Carolyn looked directly into his eyes as if she were drawing out each word. "The only way to meet this crisis," he explained, "will be by altering its character and essentially multilateralizing it. Actually, only points *e* and *h* in my article will have to be altered; the others, perhaps modified a bit, will fit perfectly." Carolyn was with him; what had Wyzanski said? "I just don't think it's workable. Nine-point programs are never workable."

After checking his in-box for any new material, Smith called in his team. Alex Gamarekian, his political-military expert, was a humorless, crewcut type on loan from the Pentagon, and had arrived at what Smith guessed was his usual hour. Franklin Harrison was one of the few Black reporters with the *Post*.

"This problem is a real gas," Harrison laughed. "Although with the world as screwed up as it is, who needs it?"

"We might as well get on with it," Smith said. "We all agreed to play, didn't we?"

"I agreed to write a *story* about it," Harrison said.

"Okay," he answered, "but are you in or out?"

"You can say I'm in."

"Look, you've been around," Smith went on. "What do you think the Chinese would be up to right now?

"Well, for starters," Harrison answered, "I'd say they'd probably like to wipe out our air bases in Thailand and take out our CIA armies."

"Good going!"

"It won't be pretty," Gamarekian warned.

"It won't," Smith agreed.

"The way I see it," Harrison said, "is that this Red Shield is supposed to be a bunch of young toughs who just got control of the neighborhood, which means they'll be full of themselves and probably pretty mean if they got the power—which they think they happen to have right now, okay? I was thinking about that this morning when I cut my face with a razor."

Smith saw the blade leaving a slit in Harrison's brown skin, which slowly filled with blood. He turned to Gamarekian. "Is there any way we could stop them?"

Gamarekian shook his head. "They'll have 120,000 troops inside Thailand in the next few days, and there's a lot more if they need them. No, they can walk through us at their own pace. That is, unless we used nukes."

"Easy does it," Harrison warned.

"That's the only way to stop those bastards!"

Harrison laughed softly to himself. "The man's got a piece." Gamarekian winced.

In a situation like this, Holmes thought, his task would be to save what he could. There had been what the game material had described as a "wanton attack"; the Thais were his clients, and supposedly, they were hurt. He had, after all, been Ambassador in Bangkok once. The Thais, he could enumerate, were genial, corrupt, kindly, evasive, epicurean, unthreatening, with flashes here and there of the European manner, or of the discipline of the Japanese. But beyond Bangkok and his official rounds, he evoked for himself the villages where he had motored weekends, with their genuinely happy round of life, apolitical, poor, self-sufficient but cheerful in some ultimate measure which had won him.

The Chinese Communists, had they indeed invaded, would have destroyed all that, the poverty, illiteracy, the physical squalor perhaps, but their spirit as well, which had made it all worthwhile. The obtrusion by the Chinese of a so-called social policy, and a sophomoric one at that, would sap the subtle spontaneity of village life, and even more the intrigue and corruption which had so fascinated him in the upper class and in the government. How could he acquiesce in the passage of a spectacle which had provided him so much entertainment? Fortunately, he reassured himself, his personal predispositions would correspond with those of his employers.

"We have," Holmes announced, "just twenty-five minutes to think of an appropriate response. We have obligations in this area." He enjoyed the shock that his unexpected gravity evoked from his two advisers.

Only one of them excited his interest. Edwin Randolph, an old Foreign Service Officer, personified the departmental mundane, and was crotchety and unpleasant to boot. But then there was Mary Watts. She was perhaps fifty, a career civil servant, whose husband was president of the ARGOS Foundation, which, Holmes suspected, was Control. She was, in her exquisite fur collar, with her open brown eyes and trim figure, altogether charming.

"If the war must come," Holmes's ancestors had said at Lexington, "let it start here." But despite this burst into militancy, he had, he knew, too much of the witty squire about him—and after all, Mary Watts was here—to keep it up. He jotted down talking points in his notebook, selected disinterestedly from his advisers and himself; gathered up his papers; and led his little tribe to the Secretary's office for their first meeting.

"I think we're all here," said the Secretary of State, glancing at his team as they seated themselves around the table.

Here again was Mansefield Vane, as elegant and commanding as he had been during the reception last night. It was not his height, Holmes noted, which drew one's attention, but the smallness of his head in relation to the verticality of his body. Or perhaps it was his almost feminine features combined with his known acuity and aggressiveness, as if he were a modern incarnation of Sir Walter Raleigh or the Earl of Essex. As a senior partner of Creighton, Watson and Vane, he had appeared during Holmes's professional life as Deputy Secretary of State, Attorney General, and briefly, in the closing months of the previous administration, in the very post which he now held in the game.

Vane began. "This military hour you've all been summoned at is not, I hope you realize, my doing. We have Control to thank for it—or, if we're to enter into the spirit of things, the Chinese Communists. You've all had a chance, I trust, to go through this morning's briefing book."

Klein glanced again at his copy.

"I should indicate the first moves that have already been taken so our lines will be clear. About a half hour ago, I received a call from the President, with the Secretary of Defense, Mr. Mikesell, already on the line. The President was eager not to appear sluggish in responding to Communist moves."

The Secretary glanced at some notes. "He has decided to issue an immediate statement along the following lines—apparently this had already been worked out with the Secretary of Defense. 'The United States and all free peoples of the world are outraged by the Chinese Communist action in Thailand. It should be noted by the Chinese Communist authorities that Thailand is allied to the United States by a treaty of mutual defense, and that the United States fully intends to honor its commitments.'" He looked up to see a raised hand. "Professor Klein?"

"Doesn't the statement radically overstress the bilateral aspect? After all, other countries might also be attacked. We should say instead, 'Military aggression is a threat to all nations.' We could then cite Article 2, paragraphs 3 and 4 of the United Nations Charter, and also," Klein added, just for good measure, "Article 51. Then we'd be covered, in case, for example, the Chinese attacked a country like Burma."

"Perhaps," the Secretary said. "However, I could see some advantages right now in not quibbling with the President."

"Exactly," said the Under Secretary, Allen Henderson, to whom everyone now turned. Henderson had gained the reputation in the Department during his many years of service of being a tough negotiator. He had pushed the U.S. line hard—in Berlin, Moscow, Beirut, Saigon, and just recently, before his retirement, in Santiago—and he had frequently won. Now he said, "The President's statement seems quite appropriate. If Burma were attacked, we would respond when it happened."

"But why wait?" Klein asked. "Why not issue a statement now which would cover us in that contingency as well?"

"Professor Klein, the effect of cutting the reference to our alliance with the Thais— that *is* what you are suggesting—would be to gut the statement of any aspect of threat. We want to scare the Chinese, not give them a lecture on the UN Charter!"

"I'm not suggesting," Klein persisted, beginning to sweat, "that we lecture the Chinese. What I'm saying is we not jump into some restrictive position before the situation is . . . What if Burma *were* attacked? We don't have a treaty with Burma."

"The fact is that Burma has not yet been attacked. Thailand has. Thailand is an ally. Isn't that clear enough? I think the President's statement expresses these facts exactly."

The Secretary intervened. "I think we can pass on—unless, Professor Klein, you have any more objections."

Klein, Holmes thought, was an obvious meddler. The game had barely begun, and already he'd shot his credit.

Something unambiguous in life: an erect cock, thought Smith.

Sansone bided his time. Let others skirmish, not Frank Sansone.

"Ambassador Holmes," the Secretary turned to him, "perhaps, as representing the bureau principally involved, you might cast some light concerning this present business."

"The facts you know," Holmes took it up. "My contribution must then lie upon some line of policy. In that regard, I should like to suggest that we do nothing at this juncture to push the Chinese into a greater militancy than they have already demonstrated. Threat, economic sanctions, large-scale military action, indeed military action in excess of recognized defense, would seem, on our part, most unwise."

"Just what exactly are you suggesting we *do*?" Henderson asked.

"Very little, so little as to test our control beyond the usual."

"Do you mean, Stoddard," Henderson kept it up, "that we just sit back and let the Chicoms take over Thailand? I needn't tell you what that would look like on the Hill." He glanced at Klein, "You might attempt to sell that around here, but I doubt you would even *try* anywhere else."

"No, no, we explode in a flurry of diplomatic activity." Holmes glanced down at his notes. "We should, by all means, seek another contact with the Soviets, and one with the Chinese in Warsaw, despite our recent failures on both counts. Our line on Thailand should be to confine the action to the frontier, if that is possible, and show our willingness to the Chinese to seek a settlement of the issues which led them to intervene, not only in Thailand, but in Indochina as well."

"I think everyone here can appreciate your restraint," Henderson said gently, "but I doubt others would, not the President, not the Hill, not the American people. Nice try, Stoddard."

"Senator Sansone," the Secretary asked, "how do *you* view the situation?"

"Well, Manse, I'm not surprised at all at what has happened. The Chinese have been insisting for years on a bigger role in the area, and now with those missiles they're supposed to have, they feel in a position to push for it. Frankly *I* feel they've got to be stopped. What I see is a meeting of the General Assembly . . ."

Smith stared down at the table. It was all pornography, like those movies which showed you things best performed in the dark, unless you were in a horny kind of mood. Sansone would lay it all out for them, the "big man!"

So the Senator agreed with him, Klein thought. Except he hadn't done his homework.

"Of course," Sansone conceded to an unidentified opponent, "we'd have to work out the details." It was true, he'd run out of things to say. All he had was the idea, but it was a hell of a lot better than nothing. Well, wasn't it?

"It seems to me," Henderson intervened, "this discussion is lacking a little realism. What we have on our hands is a full-scale war. Conferences are all very nice, but the problem right now is military. The Communists have defined it that way, and that's the way we must react to it. Our job now is to get them out of Thailand before anything else, before political settlement, before economic aid, before any inventive schemes in New York or anywhere else. I say the sooner we face up to that fact, the more realistic this discussion is going to be!"

"I'm sure," said the Secretary, glancing at Henderson over the rim of his glasses, "that the aspect of the problem to which you allude will receive at least equal time. The National Security Council meets at ten."

Smith started to light a cigarette, but his hands were shaking. He put the cigarette in his mouth unlit, and dropped his hands under the table. The whole business was obscene. The same thing was happening to him that had happened before, when he'd blown up in front of the Soviet Ambassador. He clenched his fists. The room turned white, as did the sound like that of ocean waves on sand.

Throughout the meeting an angel sat next to Michael Klein, its large, dusty and somewhat greasy wing right next to his shoulder. It might have been a stone angel, serene and immobile, but instead, it was fidgety and nervous. If it would only leave him alone— but it was constantly rubbing him with its wing, perhaps leaving marks on his suit.

It seems to me, Klein rehearsed to himself, that the only way to meet this crisis is through a multilateral approach.

Who shall go for us? the angel had asked in a querulous voice.

Klein sighed.

Who? the angel demanded again.

Klein would explain his entire plan, *a* though *i*, though they wouldn't listen, they would humiliate him in some way, okay, okay?

"It seems to me," Klein said, "that the only way to meet this crisis is through a multilateral approach. A few months ago, I published an article containing a plan for the internationalization of Southeast Asia which might just work if it were put through in the proper way. Point *a* would be the convening of an international conference of all countries in the area, and all interested outside countries, the U.S., the Soviets, China, the U.K., France, and so on. Point *b* would be the creation of a permanent Secretariat with broad powers to . . ."

Henderson cut him off. "At this point, Professor Klein, the best possible procedure would be to circulate your plan as a staff study, suitably revised, I suggest, to take into account the particularities of the problem we are discussing here. There is a danger of anticipating too much, like the eager young political officer arriving at his first post with his reports already written."

"Meanwhile," the Secretary interposed, "we should solemnly pray that the Chinese—all billion of them—might drown themselves in the sea like lemmings."

"You've just wished away half my clientele," Holmes said in mock horror.

"Actually," the Secretary resumed, "in the discussion we've just had—at this point I may perhaps be guilty of an act of faith—I can see the beginnings of an approach. Some scissors and paste, and I suspect we'll have something for the NSC."

It was a nudge toward consensus, Klein thought, but did it mean that now no part of his article would be considered? When there was no crisis, there would be no pressure to really do anything. Plans like his would be shelved. And when there *was* a crisis, there would be no time, except to muddle through. Bastard Henderson!

He'd have given them a plan on a silver platter. If they didn't want it, fuck 'em! Shortsightedness was an endemic factor in the Department of State, for which *he* wasn't responsible. It would be amusing, when he'd left the game, to describe meetings like this.

He'd be standing in the center of a little group of his colleagues. He'd been asked to be a player, which they hadn't been. They couldn't fail, despite their jibes, to be interested, and envious. The game was invaluable, but it was amusing, too; he'd be deft, perhaps a little cruel. It was a microcosm, a human comedy under glass.

Klein's musings were broken by a Control officer turning on a television set. It flickered for a moment, and when the screen had cleared, there appeared in a khaki uniform a slim brown man with a tiny mustache. A microphone was being held up to his mouth, like a rag soaked in chloroform. Under the picture was an identification: *Colonel Dhanamitt, Army of Thailand.* "The Chinese claim to come in peace," he said, "but is it peace, I ask you, to invade another country?"

Then the voice of the interviewer. "Are Thai troops putting up any resistance?"

"In this sector we have very few men."

"When do you estimate you will have reinforcements?"

"I understand that the Americans are already here, and that thousands of American paratroopers will arrive very soon and darken the skies."

"How far have the Chinese already advanced since they crossed . . ?"

The poor son-of-a-bitch, thought Smith.

Fantastic! You had to hand it to them, thought Sansone.

The cave of shadows, Klein smirked.

Why not? Holmes mused.

The Control Officer distributed a telegram from the U.S. Mission to the United Nations. It contained the request from the Thais for an emergency meeting of the Security Council at 4 p.m.

An hour later Sansone stumbled out of the meeting, blinking

from the change of light. A lot of talk, but what had it come to? The Secretary had simply ended it: "The UN, of course, is a tactic which we could use if events turned that way. As for the military side, we shall have to see what the snapping turtles from the other bank have to say." That was it! He'd gotten hardly a hint of a guideline. And the UN would be meeting in just a few hours!

He tried to imagine his stomach, liver, the turnings of his intestines, which now ached. Once he'd let his son, Giorgio, put his head on his belly to listen; how they'd laughed together. Celestial harmony!

As Sansone walked out of the men's room, Wylie Adams told him, "It reminds me of a trip I once took on the old *President Taylor*. We left port waving, drinking champagne, got just out of the harbor, and had to put back with engine trouble."

"I'm not giving up on our idea of a UN conference," Sansone insisted. "Because sooner or later they're going to need a policy, and then they'll be coming back to us begging for it. Right now all we've got to do is work up some language that puts the Security Council behind getting the Chinese out of there." Sometimes Sansone admired his own politician's ease with defeats. You lost here, you lost there, but you didn't make each time a test of the world's worth. He sat in his office lining up a row of boxes on his notepad; then he'd *x* them off.

Smith couldn't call Sally Jenks, not now. The morning stretched out in front of him the way it used to before he had time for long coffee breaks or half hours with his wife. Now he was back to the same murderous schedule, only it lacked the fatality of the real world. Yet there'd be the same series of confrontations, papers, meetings, deadlines, and so the same nervous edge he must push to get everything done.

He'd been proud once of having it all to do, but there had always been, in those days when he had power, too many people and too many countries. He had constantly to be flying and putting down here and there for meetings at airports, with the engines kept running. A last-minute attempt at familiarity, at something personal, and the plane would be leaving the ground. It would come to him then that he had probably not been clear, or that he had failed in the business he'd come to do. But more—that everything had been forced and artificial, and that the man on the ground now doubted him.

The more he'd become a spokesman for the United States, the more the country itself had slipped away. He could not imagine it anymore, except in picture postcards or in views from a plane window. How could a man live in Shreveport, Louisiana, and work for an auto-parts distributor, as Sally's brother, Wally, did, while Zach's plane glided over the weather and would put down in Prague in thirty-five minutes? Were newspapers true, did the people in them really exist, were there Blacks who rioted, and a little boy from Rochester whose dog had fallen down a well?

And so he loved Sally Jenks beyond imagination, her funny gestures, her putterings and slang, her dreams, and the rhythm of her body, the rhythm he had found only in her. He could almost feel it now, that abstract, lyric, pulsating, beyond-rivers'-reach-calm; he wanted it now!

"You said you didn't know soul music, 'member, when we first met? But you do now, you big stuffed shirt, course you do. Want to dance?"

When could he call her?

Mary Watts, thought Holmes, should have lived in an age when women carried fans. Her derisive manner suggested Oscar Wilde and lawn parties, subtlety, innuendo, an intricate etiquette. "May I presume we have something to say?" is all she'd asked. Her silver punch ladle, Holmes mused, dipped at 'presume,' then peaked at 'say.'

"Just what *are* we proposing?" his aide, Edwin Randolph, asked.

Holmes sighed, and passed his hand over the top of his head, barely covered with a few strands of white hair. "My dear fellow, we are officials of the Department of State. Our role is not to decide policy, but to wait for others more decisive than ourselves to decide it for us."

☆ ☆ ☆

White: World Monitoring Service, Peking, December 7, 1846 hours, Flash Transcription

OFFICIAL USE ONLY

Statement of Shih-Ying CHEN, Acting Chairman of the Central Committee of the People's Republic of China

We of the Central Committee of the People's Republic of China send this statement to the capitalist and revisionist powers: An end must now come to all forms of imperialism in Southeast Asia. The old colonialist empires are finished. The British, the French, and the Dutch have mostly given up the game because they proved too weak to resist the iron will of the peoples. In recent years, the United States has established a new imperialist empire. In some areas, this domination is maintained by full military occupation. Confident of its power, including nuclear weapons, the American military-industrial clique has worked its will unchallenged.

The peoples of Southeast Asia, in fraternity with the People's Republic of China, now rise up to throw out the American imperialists. We are armed with the most powerful weapons, and, for the first time, we possess nuclear rockets capable of destroying the major cities of the imperialist aggressors. We are not afraid to use these weapons in the cause of freedom.

Let the American capitalists beware lest their cities be burnt to ashes. We demand the immediate departure of all imperialist forces, including advisers and intelligence spies, from all countries of Southeast Asia. We will resist with force, including nuclear arms, any attempt by the foreign powers to control or oppress any country in this part of the world; and we extend to all exploited peoples our aid in their struggles for freedom.

White: World Monitoring Service, Peking, December 7, 1915 hours, Flash Transcription

OFFICIAL USE ONLY

Proclamation of the Central Committee, People's Republic of China

At the direction of the Central Committee, forces of the People's Republic of China have today entered Thailand at the fervent plea of the Thai people.

A lot of big talk, Sansone thought after he had read the Chinese statement. A thick-set, fat-lipped man with his arms crossed on his chest, Mussolini had drained the Pontine Marshes, but what else had he done? It had all been talk.

Sansone had visited his uncle in Catanzaro, a tailor, a barber, a road worker when there was work. His uncle lived in a little town built up in the mountains off the road to avoid the tax collectors. His uncle had seen Mussolini once, but the town, that ancient town so deep in brown stone it could sweat rain, when it rained, for days after, continued its daily life. What difference had Mussolini made with his big talk?

But the invasion of Thailand was a fact. It was a measure of his being an American that Frank Sansone could dismiss talk and weigh

63

facts. Eighty-five missiles. How dangerous could those be when America had forty times as many, and in hardened sites, with electronic decoys, the book had said? Hot air. He wouldn't be bluffed out by a bunch of stupid-ass students. That's all they were. Students who didn't do anything, but talk!

The UN—that was a ghost world. He was Italian enough to know how to make a *bella figura* in the UN. But the real issues were military force, economic power. To forget that was to believe one's own speeches.

Martha buzzed him. Who walked in but Tucker McGrath! There he was! Sansone sprang up from his seat, and hugged his old aide until Tucker began to gasp. "Glad to see you, boss," Tucker said— what he'd always called him. Together they'd draft a speech that'd knock the socks off the Chinese!

☆ ☆ ☆

"Interesting," Franklin Harrison said, after he'd read the Chinese statement. "The Soviets seem off the hook."

"What about the reference," Smith asked, "to the 'revisionist powers'?"

"Maybe just a conditioned reflex. Can't tell." Harrison went on. "The Soviets might feel a whole lot safer in the long run just dealing with the Chinese out there. Their game could be deeper than we think."

"Do you think the Soviets and Chinese have a deal going?" Smith asked the *Post* reporter.

"You mean Iran?" Harrison asked. "Well, why not, my man?"

☆ ☆ ☆

To Klein, the Chinese statement indicated a wider design, something he had predicted. But some people couldn't see farther than their own noses. What the Chinese demanded, it had been clear to him from the beginning, was an adjustment of relative influence—

but this, as he'd already said, could only be absorbed in a larger multilateral structure. Carolyn Carr smiled to herself as if there were something amusing in what he'd said. He'd prefer she just listen like a graduate student in his seminar in International Law.

"It seems to me that a multi-issue approach seems called for now," Holmes told his staff. "Perhaps we shall call in Klein with his celebrated article, though I hope we can assume control for tactics. He has a certain solipsism about being right, which means he must be used rather carefully."

His buzzer sounded. "The Thais are here. How fun! Should we have Klein over, if we can squeeze him in before the NSC? Oh, why not? Frieda, could you ask Professor Klein to join us in, say, half an hour? And could you ask him to send over some reprints of his article right away? I'm sure he has them."

It was Ney! The Thai diplomat stood before him in his blue suit. So they'd chosen *him* for the part of Ambassador Atthakor. Did Holmes notice a faint smile on his lips, as they exchanged initial pleasantries?

When Ney sat in the capacious leather chair, he seemed completely lost. Indeed, he seemed hardly to be there at all, except for a light, charming, insinuating voice, which repeated like a bird, 'What can you do, coo-coo, for us?' How well he knew his part!

As the Thai Ambassador, Ney would have felt that all that military might, which Holmes or the Secretary represented, could somehow save them. He wouldn't think what happens when America fights a war, how it burns and scars and wrecks. "I cannot tell you," Holmes said to him ironically, although almost as if it were true, almost as if Ney were a stranger to him, "how personally concerned I am, how many dear friends I have in Thailand."

"Yes, yes . . ?" Ney gave no hint of recognition.

"Even if we fought the Chinese together, as we apparently are doing now, there would be great suffering."

"We are not afraid to die for our country."

"The Thai people are very brave and could, I am sure, make their name a byword for courage. I am only thinking, Mr. Ambassador—and, I hasten to say, it is my personal opinion only, as our position is still being formulated"—was he actually saying this?—"that perhaps some adjustments might be preferable to an extended war, some limited acceptance of Chinese leadership in the area. I personally feel that this might be preferable to an extended ground war, a Korea or Vietnam, which would leave your country in ashes."

"There are many things we must consider in this problem. We must 'entertain all the options,' as you say."

"I was merely suggesting one."

"Yes, it could be considered, I am sure, with all the others." Ney suddenly looked into his eyes. "One alternative, Mr. Holmes, would be the nuclear weapons with which you are armed and which, we assume, you carry for the purpose of protecting your bases, and implicitly for protecting your allies as well."

"It is our fervent hope," Holmes parried—Ney or Ambassador Atthakor wasn't missing a trick—"that such weapons will not be used, that we will be able to handle the question diplomatically. We are presently exploring the notion of a conference, starting with the premise that any longer-range solution to the problems in the area must take into account the reality of Chinese power."

"But it will be clear to your President, will it not, that if nuclear weapons *are* used, the Chinese will be forced to leave? Is that not our common objective, your government's and mine?"

"Indeed," Holmes replied, "but the use of nuclear weapons is a Pandora's box . . ."

"A pox?"

Holmes threw up his hands. Ney would know what that phrase meant, but would Ambassador Atthakor? He continued. "We would not wish to save Thailand, or, shall I put it more succinctly, its present government, at the risk of laying waste to the entire countryside." He paused, stared away. "Well, sir, let us call you when we know more here."

"Don't call us, we'll call you, as you say."

"Quite." Holmes rose and extended his hand, which was almost as delicate as the Thai's. It had been Maynard Keynes, he remembered, who had studied hands, and had decided that Franklin Roosevelt's resembled those of the British Foreign Secretary, Lord Grey, of a still earlier time.

Zach Smith came out from behind his desk to greet the British Ambassador, Sir Harold Beckwyth-Pearce, G.M.C., C.V.O. As a close ally, the United Kingdom must be in on the game, and taking it quite seriously, as Sir Harold was playing himself. Smith was alone, having set his aides, Hawley and Harrison, to cranking up NATO.

"Harold, how are you?" Smith heartily grasped his hand. Sir Harold was one of those interchangeable British diplomats one met in a career who seemed technically competent (they could transmit a clear message) and yet were vague to the point of disappearance. There were clearly things he believed in. Had he lived in the era of Lord Kitchener, he would gladly have trooped to the colors, been shot or gassed in the trenches, and gone at it again and again, until he was either dead or sufficiently maimed to have had all his protestations overruled. What Smith missed was a touchable depth. Habits and tics Sir Harold had in profusion, but personality Smith had been unable to find.

When they had first met fifteen years ago in Bucharest, it had been necessary to find something to be social about, because one couldn't be social about business, so they had decided on the war. Sir Harold had spent most of it as a liaison officer to the Arabs, usually behind German lines. He had stories to tell, but although the stories came up frequently, Smith could never quite find the point of them. They were all allusions, quips, and sly asides, and seemed to fade away in a haze of modesty or reticence. It was a manner which Smith found easy to slide into himself, so that nothing ever came of the stories he told either. They would spend ten or fifteen minutes on the war, and then get down to work. Today, Smith decided to be straight and play the game.

"Harold, what I'd like for you to tell me is just what the Chinese are up to."

"Oh, dear," Sir Harold sighed, "I was hoping you could tell *me*. I'm afraid this visit has been a frightful mistake, a blunder of the first water."

The coffee arrived. "Our ambassador in Warsaw, Marshall Peters, got nothing from the Chinese just as little as a week ago."

"Sorry about that. We've had as little luck ourselves. Our embassy at Peking is practically closed." Sir Harold took out his cigarette case, then thought better of it, and put it back. "Zachariah, I came here seeking genuine enlightenment. My personal opinion—would you like my personal opinion? I'm afraid, poor thing, it is all I have."

Smith wondered what game Sir Harold was playing. "Of course."

"Well, I guess this time the Chinese would be serious about kicking us out."

Smith showed him the Chinese proclamation. It confirmed "most definitely" what Sir Harold already thought.

Smith had given him nothing; the information would probably be waiting for him when Sir Harold returned to the embassy. But now, Smith decided to pass the British information of some value. He had no authorization, but might have gotten it had he applied. And, he thought, the British would have received the information from us eventually. Would he *really* have done this? Yes.

"We have hard information, Harold." He could not shake the feeling that everything he said was in italics. "I want this strictly held, because I am going beyond my authority with this, that the Chinese can now deliver about eighty-five ICBMs." He read aloud from his briefing book while Sir Harold scrawled notes: location, probable performance capabilities, range, megatonnage, guidance, site vulnerability. "You understand, these are mostly just educated guesses. And, of course, we don't know the targeting, though I expect London and the Gloucester sites would be on the list."

"Hmm. Thank you, thank you. Of course, we knew they had been testing. This is very good indeed. Yes, quite good. Zachariah, I shall treat this as an emanation from sparrows. I appreciate your confidence."

"I always suspected you had another channel through which to pass this kind of stuff."

"Did you? Well, it *is* more secure." He actually gave a little wink.

"Harold, it would be absolutely vital for us both to know as much as possible about what's going on. I would have been sticking my neck out rather far."

"Yes, I can appreciate that. I wish I could reciprocate, Zachariah, I wish I could. I do have something. There is a political type in the Soviet Far East Bureau . . ."

"Could you give me his name? The harder the better right now."

"Careful. It's Feodor Osipov. He's supposed to be a rather nice chap, so if you would treat the matter . . ."

"Of course."

"I'm told he talks rather freely to one of our First Secs. Says the Presidium have a new China policy, that, in essence, they are now quite relaxed about Chinese expansionism, as long as it is southerly. That, in fact, they have all but agreed to give the Chinese a free hand."

"In exchange for what?"

"He thought the decision might well be economic, or possibly a concession to pro-Chinese rumblings in the Warsaw Pact." Sir Harold glanced down at his briefing book. "Here's something. Do you know about Kuznetsov's trip to Peking?"

"Actually, we do. But what would the Soviets get out of letting the Chinese walk over Southeast Asia?"

"I don't know. A free hand in Eastern Europe, Cuba, Latin America . . ."

"Or Iran?" Smith asked.

"Yes, that could be it, but this is hardly an area of the world where the Chinese could affect the issue one way or another."

"Are the Soviets on the move because they think we're tied up elsewhere?"

"Quite possibly."

But then Harold seemed to want to go. Smith leaned back in his chair; he would play once more. "Oh, how I wish we were still a colony, and could let you fellows run the world."

"I think we've lost our nerve, and we're broke. Now we're reduced to playing little games!" Another minute, and Sir Harold had gone. Smith went through the motions of a chit to Henderson, a telegram to Moscow.

"Of course, the article will have to be revised," Klein told Holmes, once their staffs had been introduced. "I was looking it over just a few minutes ago, but still I thought . . . Do you think the general approach is sound?"

"Yes, on the whole. I agree"—Holmes spoke from notes—"that we should have a general conference sponsored by the UN; that an international secretariat should be established; that we should acquiesce in a predominant, though not exclusive, Chinese role in the security of the area—more on that later; that all foreign troops should be excluded. I do not agree with the blanket exclusion of advisers. I also disagree with the creation of a Southeast Asian political council, as it would look too much like a Peking Pact."

"No, no, I agree, of course. But don't you think some kind of regional council makes sense?"

Holmes paused before Klein's obsequiousness. Was this the other side of his natural arrogance? Why did Jews always have to be so ill at ease? He and Klein talked around some of the points. There simply wasn't time to get anything to the Secretary before the NSC.

Smith rode to the meeting with Allen Henderson and a Control officer named Ellsworth Pruitt. If Pruitt were suddenly to reveal to him that he were made up of plastic overlays, like a Pentagon briefing or an anatomy model, Smith wouldn't be surprised. Would Pruitt bleed? Probably. Everyone did. It was something dependable, almost reassuring.

Smith said nothing. Henderson had read his chit about Sir Harold's Soviet contact, Osipov, but the information wouldn't be hard. Kremlin gossip like that was always fairly cheap, although Osipov was apparently no clerk. Smith, just on a hunch, had checked Biographic Intelligence in the Administration Office. Sure enough, Osipov had been there. Smith had given Henderson a few particulars from the report, but Henderson had probably dismissed the whole thing.

He saw again that Henderson, like himself, was a handsome man. But where Smith was still boyish in appearance, Henderson looked grave and responsible, with silver temples, heavy eyebrows, craggy features. He looked tough and credible, where Smith seemed brash and flashy. If Smith had been a woman, he would have been . . . an airline hostess, not a whore, not a whore like . . . Why doesn't that bastard say something?

"We're going into this meeting," Smith finally said, "and we don't even have a position."

"And it worries you, as I suppose it should."

"Well, yes. Doesn't it worry you?"

Henderson sighed. "We'll just have to work something out, won't we?"

Smith made a nervous shrug and before he knew it, Henderson had put his arm on his shoulder. He didn't need that bastard's arm; he was doing fine! Henderson was actually kneading his shoulder with his hand. Smith twisted away. He was on the payroll just like Henderson!

☆ ☆ ☆

The Secretary's team mounted the stone stairs of the Executive Office Building, that corniced wonder of nineteenth-century solemnity and exuberance which once had housed the old Department of State. It had outlasted all efforts to tear it down.

Greek, Roman, Egyptian, the buildings of Washington were phony and timeless. In the moonlight or at early dawn, they almost fooled you, but not by day.

As a young man, Smith had once paddled a canoe down the Potomac. As he drifted into the city, he'd imagined the banks, marshy or lightly forested, sprinkled with Indians, under a slower rhythm. Dip and slide, he saw the only mirror crack the sky.

As they walked, a wind blew down Pennsylvania Avenue catching their coats, touching their ankles. The traffic was moving. There was no history in Washington, no tradition to work through, as at Whitehall, or the Quai d'Orsay, or the halls of the Kremlin. A counter against history, one was always young in Washington, powerful and vaguely irresponsible.

The Executive Office Building set a different scene. It suggested a more gracious if somewhat cynical view of the world, a return to an older style of diplomacy. Its demands were not coercive; only that it offered a subtle resistance, like a Stradivarius, which almost imperceptibly shakes when its violinist plays a false note.

The Secretary of Defense had already arrived, and with him, his Under Secretary and the Chairman of the Joint Chiefs. Next came the Secretary of the Treasury; Wally Perkins of the U.S.I.A.; and the Vice President, a former senator from Tennessee, who sat like a great stone eminence. To Frank Sansone, the Vice President was "Harry" and an old colleague. And Sansone had known Wally Perkins a million years ago, when Wally had been Washington editor of the old *American* before it was bought out.

"Bad situation, Wally. You guys got it all figured out?"

"Not yet, but I'm having fun, I suppose."

"Why, 'I suppose'?"

"Oh, you know, Frank . . ."

"It all feels like work to me."

"It *looks* like work," Wally said. "I hear the President hasn't made up his mind on anything yet, so he'll be . . ."

"Frank," the Vice President signaled to Sansone, "give me a ring, if you get a chance later in the day, just to chat."

"Okay, Harry, love to."

Smith picked out his old commanding officer in the Strategic Air Command, General George Curtis, now playing the Chairman of the Joint Chiefs. "You warming up the engines, General?"

"Frankly, Smith, a pre-emptive strike"—Curtis actually lowered his voice—"strictly conventional, would knock those Chinese nuclear facilities right off the map. Might be the safest move at this point in time."

"Sounds like you want a major war."

"What do you think we got now, boy? That statement this morning, the one from the Chicom High Command, what's that but a declaration of war? Not in so many words, but that's the situation. Remember the bombing run on Poloesti? I was on that strike, Smith. 1943. We weren't afraid to use what we had to get an advantage *then*, seize the high ground, as my colleagues would say, no, sir. Those people wouldn't face up to us in a real war, don't you guys across the river kid yourselves about that."

"Okay, but what about the Soviets?"

"My view, Smith, is that if we limited ourselves to a strictly surgical strike—you got that?—well, I think they'd back down."

Holmes spoke to no one, but stood as insubstantial as a Proustian ghost.

Mitchell Murray entered flanked by his foreign policy expert, Morris Friedlander, and by Cronin Brown of the CIA. Like Richard III, "deep between two divines," thought Holmes. There was the President, in the flesh, as it were, or the almost-President, had a few states gone the other way in the last election. Like a president, he dissolved into his images, in this case, a triple M ("Mitchell Murray from Madison"), as on a tin can. Or that famous photograph of Murray waving to a crowd, reproduced a million times, like reflections in facing mirrors. Or his way, often imitated or parodied, of putting questions into the voice of the average citizen: "What does that have to do with sending my kids to college?" Or that gesture with the side of his hand with which he cut his phrases, as his father had cut meat with a cleaver in Madison. Without this packaging—and there were other boxes and labels—he would hardly have been conceivable. Perhaps inside there was nothing but a small boy, a tow-headed caterpillar who had begun spinning before anyone knew to look.

"Good morning, good morning, gentlemen." The man exuded a heartiness which would have been refreshing, had it been genuine. "I think we can all get started." He was either credible or not. Smith's mind flipped back and forth, as with an ambiguous gestalt.

"Manse, they are shooting this portion, aren't they?" The President motioned to the camera crew. "You fellows ready?" He cleared his throat and faced the cameras. "Before we begin, I want to say that we need to work together, be of one mind even if we disagree, be of one mind in our devotion to the interests of our great nation and to the cause of freedom. In this exercise, we will be facing a major international crisis. With your skill and determination, we will learn how better to face future crises, and so achieve the peace for which we all strive."

He motioned again to the camera crew. "Got that? Well, okay then, turn off the cameras." He turned to his team around the table. "Well, I don't have to tell you gentlemen—you've all read the cables— we're in a real pickle. I've been thinking of nothing else since Control got me up early this morning, so early I felt I was getting up with the Chinese Communists rather than with normal people like ourselves." Everyone laughed at the role play, and then, as if a lens had moved over the entire scene, it became real. What difference did it make? Holmes asked himself, and for just a moment felt a twinge of panic.

"Mr. Mikesell, who gets up even earlier than they do, is going to map out the military situation." The President gave him a nod. "Mike?"

Everything was going as planned, Smith noted. There was the Secretary of Defense, standing by an easel holding plastic overlays of Southeast Asia. It showed great red arrows penetrating borders, solid and cross-hatched areas of sure and dubious control, numerical designations of will-to-resist, graphs displaying troops and materiel, kill ratios, cost estimates. It was, Smith imagined, like a corporate board meeting on how a competitor had penetrated a favored market, and what it might cost to get him out.

Mikesell's voice was flat yet energetic, with none of the class of the Secretary of State's. "The 12th and 23rd Chinese Communist Route Armies are sweeping in here from the north. Friendly forces, U.S. and Thai, are represented by these arrows here." Mikesell put his pointer down. "The situation, gentlemen, is not encouraging. Numbers of troops, however, are not the only factor. Armaments are another." He flipped over another sheet on the easel. "Together they establish what we call the KREC index."

"The KREC Index?" asked Mansefield Vane. "What kind of term is that?"

"That's the Kill Ratio in an Expectable Confrontation. Now if we factor in the KREC Index . . ."

"Excuse me," Smith broke in. "At this point, aren't the Chinese supposed to have missile capability?"

"There is a zero risk," Mikesell answered, "that a Chinese first strike could kill even a few U.S. cities. Once their missiles are released, they will be neutralized by our ABM system."

Smith smiled to himself at the President of Midwest Aerospace, who was now playing the Secretary of Defense. In the military, he knew, no system was one hundred percent effective. The components malfunctioned, the personnel goofed, the orders never arrived, or they arrived garbled or wrong. All the while, the officials in charge would go on record that the system worked perfectly.

"In any case," Mikesell continued, "the Chinese missile force can probably be neutralized by strong counterforce threats. Of course, what we have to be concerned with right here is the situation in Northern Thailand. Unless we can radically alter the KREC index,

I'm afraid we can't hold that ground. The only way we know to do that is to employ tactical nuclear weapons."

"Tactical nuclear weapons?" Smith exclaimed.

"The fact is," General Curtis intervened, "tactical nuclear weapons are the equivalent of strategic bombing with conventional bombs."

"Oh, come on!"

"And it could be argued"—Mikesell shot Smith a disdainful look—"if we had not intended to use them under certain foreseeable circumstances, such as we are facing right now, we wouldn't have deployed them."

When would the Secretary of State intervene? Smith waited, and then went on. "Suppose," he insisted, "the Chinese are determined not to lose, or they consider tactical weapons too much a provocation? What's to keep them from launching those eighty-five missiles they're supposed to have? That ABM system of yours is supposed to work a hundred percent, but you know damn well it won't."

"As I've already said . . ." the Secretary of Defense began.

"You know it's never been tested!"

The President motioned. "See here, Smith, see here. We can't allow ourselves to be blackmailed every time some nation rattles a few rockets. What would our friends say if every time we were threatened and, gentlemen, this is the kind of thing that is going to happen more and more. Well, they would say, and rightly so, 'You can't stick to your agreements.' And what would the American people say, or Congress, for that matter, if we turned tail and ran because the Chinese blustered a bit with what I gather are some still rather primitive weapons?"

"Mr. President, that new regime in China—what if they're fools enough to *use* those weapons?" Smith turned to Mikesell. "You know the ABM system won't work, you've always known that!" Would he have talked this way in a *real* meeting, with a *real* President?

"I supposes the point you are making, Zach," Henderson smirked, "is that an undependable adversary who's got nuclear weapons can do anything he wants."

"No, I'm not. But to see this fight in purely military terms seems a mistake to me." The Secretary of State was looking down at his papers. "We have to ask," Smith persisted, "what are the Chinese objectives?"

"To communize Asia, I suspect," said the CIA's Cronin Brown, as if slipping his words from a poison ring.

"Okay, okay. But suppose they want to gain friendly or even somewhat dependent states, but not necessarily expand their territory." Well, it was clear enough. "Then we might deal with the Chinese in some better way than risking a nuclear exchange, which could mean ten to fifteen million dead!" He would stand up and shout, he would press his black hands against the walls!

"Mr. President, I hesitate," Holmes said, "to project what is already a bad situation. Indeed, one might almost accuse Control of being lurid in their imagination. But in any case, it merits perhaps a moment's pause to consider the consequences should we be indeed forced to use these weapons."

Henderson broke in. "In my experience, the use of force has always been an option—which is why, Stoddard, we have these weapons."

"Then why *not* use them?"

The Secretary of State looked at him with total incredulity. "Stoddard, just what are you talking about?"

"It might spice things up a little bit around here. For over twenty years, we've resisted the temptation. But now I say, do it, incinerate them, let's get back that old feeling we had at Hiroshima and Nagasaki!"

"Don't get smart, Holmes!" Henderson snapped. "We're talking about options here. In the final analysis, we must live up to our agreements with the Thais, and if that means tactical weapons, then that's the option we must be prepared to exercise!"

Vane stared directly at the President, then slowly shifted his eyes until he ended up staring at Henderson. "Do you think if we actually used those weapons, it would be so quickly forgotten? There has been operating since World War II a certain unsigned treaty that these weapons will not be used! We are alive today because of that agreement. I say we must not use them unless we are backed to the wall! Do I make myself clear, Mr. Henderson?"

"All right, all right," said the President. "Suppose we went ahead with a *threat* to use these smaller tactical weapons. Isn't it a threat we've always made? It's nothing new, nothing at all. I don't think I'd be open to the charge of being the first. And besides, the actual strength of these weapons is roughly the same as regular strategic bombing, except it's somewhat more concentrated. Isn't that true?"

"That's right," said General Curtis. "You can rest assured about that. And if we use those weapons, we will be in the best possible position at this point . . ."

"What do you think the likelihood is that I . . . that we would have to use them?"

Mikesell spoke. "It is, as you say, Mr. President, a threat we've always maintained. And we haven't used them yet."

"I am again much less confident," said Secretary of State Vane, "as this is a situation in which fighting is already occurring."

"Mr. President," Under Secretary of Defense Palmerston intervened— had he been recruited from Mikesell's corporate staff or from the Pentagon?—"there are some military facts here. We have very few troops in the area, only about eleven thousand. To get other combat units up there would take at least ten days. Two weeks is more likely. We're talking here about two or three divisions, at least, if we want to hold the areas cleared by those weapons."

"Well, in *that* case, maybe we'd better hold *off* on the nuclear business," said the President, "until those men can get up there. Maybe we should just sit it out for awhile." He nodded to Mikesell.

"Mr. President, on further consideration we feel the matter needs additional study. We'll have a report on that matter next meeting."

"Fine, let's see that report." Murray's face stiffened. "How many men can we get up there in the next few days?"

"We'll get as many as we can, as fast as we can," General Curtis said, "but . . ."

"I don't want any last-ditch stands. This isn't a suicide mission. I want them up there to slow the Chinese down, got that?"

"Yes, sir. But are you saying, sir, that we are *not* to use the nukes, even though our men will be armed with them, until we have enough troops up there to occupy the ground?"

"That's right." The President gave a decisive nod, and then said nothing for about fifteen seconds. "I've got to get a statement out in the next hour"—Morris Friedlander looked up—"for delivery early this afternoon. That meeting at the UN, Frank, the Security Council, what are we going to do about *that*?"

Sansone blinked his eyes—had he been daydreaming? "Well, my idea is we go for a UN force through the Security Council, and . . ."

"They'll veto that in two minutes," Henderson said.

"Right, I know they'll veto it! And then we'll go for a full conference at the UN to air things out, and . . ."

"I think I better get out that statement."

"Mr. President, I'm not finished yet!"

"Mr. President," Vane came in, "the Senator . . ."

"I need to get that statement out to the American people. I better get on with it. Now, Manse, I want you to look into that conference at the UN. Christ, what kind of policy have I got? I wanted agreement, and, goddamn it, I got nothing! The hell with this!"

The meeting would resume at two-thirty that afternoon at State, this time without the President.

Even though he had not been invited to the NSC meeting, Klein thought, *Holmes* would use him. But even if he did, why was he always *used*? He was, he realized, almost grateful. But why didn't he use others? Why not lead? Staff and line. He was so distinctly staff, had always been staff. Even in the army, he'd been given a staff job, had never commanded troops. Couldn't he have done it as well as anyone else?

The Legal Advisor—a Jewish job. He was not an anti-defamation type, but hadn't it mattered in *his* life in the subtlest way? Staff, the Legal Advisor, the court Jew?

In Israel, there were Jewish line officers, Jewish troops, all armed with Sten guns. It was only possible because they had once again become the militant people of the Bible, before history had twisted them up in the Diaspora, and he had lost his confidence.

Would that explain it, that sponge of time he could squeeze out over his own inadequacy? Screw them! He had the ideas, and they would come to him, as Holmes already had. And if they didn't, they would revert to inert matter, burn like overturned cars! He had the ideas, the models, the morphology of time, so that even if they didn't, he held the future . . . because he had thought of it!

As he rode back in the limo, it occurred to Smith that the question of Soviet intentions had never come up. But wasn't it essential? The Soviets were fostering a revolt in Northern Iran, Kuznetsov was in Peking right now, and nobody had even mentioned them! Would the whole thing have to blow up in their faces before they realized what the Soviets were up to? Game or no game, he was going to find out!

It would be interesting what the Soviet Ambassador had to say. Vane would be gracious, but Smith would put the screws to him—the objectionable Mr. Smith.

In Moscow, the KGB had tailed him around bumper to bumper, and had even followed him into the men's rooms, as if to measure equipment. Confrontation of East and West: seven inches versus six inches. But gentlemen, six inches of truth versus seven inches of lies!

Sansone stared out the car window at the poplar trees now standing bare along Constitution Avenue. He remembered their rustling leaves once flashing past in the sun, like the spangles of a woman's dress. Halcyon days, whatever halcyon meant. He felt himself in pieces, put together with tubes and shafts and cranks, which leaked, which broke. He'd got nothing at the meeting; the President had completely ignored him.

Back at his office, he found the game's UN Ambassador, Hiram Kirkland, on the phone. As a former candidate for the vice-presidential nomination, and a senator from Connecticut, Kirkland was an old associate. Sansone had always found him vain and imperious, but that had never gotten in the way of politics. Now he settled back in his swivel chair for a pleasant chat, but—it seemed incredible—Kirkland was bawling him out for not telling him what was going on. He was actually angry!

"Come on, Hiram. I just got back from the NSC myself, and before then, we didn't even *have* a policy. Although I'm not sure we have one now."

"I could have rung up Manse, or the President myself, for that matter. This is nonsense!"

He went on and on; he seemed to be taking it all so seriously. Maybe Kirkland had been playing the game too long. Sansone took a deep breath, then smiled to himself. "I know you've had a hard morning, too, and I can appreciate what you have to go through up there with a hundred countries, or how many there are by now, screaming at you."

As Sansone was describing the National Security Council meeting, Kirkland broke in, "I was afraid this was going to happen. We need to review the entire situation out there in Southeast Asia. Not just from the point of view of evading decisions, but of actually trying to solve some problems. What *I* propose is to hold a UN conference on the entire situation. Of course, I can see difficulties right now with the Chinese occupying Thailand, but speaking to you quite frankly, that might be a good thing, it might actually make us face up to a few things."

"Like what?"

"That we can't be the world's policeman. What do you think I mean?"

Sansone grinned. "Hiram, you're right, you're absolutely right about your idea for a UN conference. It's brilliant. Why don't you send a telegram, or something, so it can be cranked into the wheelworks down here. Or better yet, why don't you call the President? I'll back you."

"I just may."

"What do you make of the Soviets?"

Kirkland started talking in a way that sounded to Sansone just a bit odd. Of course, Hiram had been up to New York, too, and they used to say the UN never changed. "Ambassador Federov, last night at the Egyptian embassy, he was, oh, his usual charming self. A few gross remarks about our hostess, a few snide asides about his cronies in the Warsaw Pact. I was fending off Gladys Rolston of the American Friends of the UN, no friends of mine, doing my best to do my duty. But I did manage to observe, *en passant,* to His Excellency that we were rather worried by all those troops and hardware the Chinese had collected on the Thai border. Federov merely shrugged with a boys-will-be-boys look which elicited from me just a slightly irritated, 'Doesn't it worry you?' And then, Frank, I brought up Iran. He shook his head, and then scooted, leaving me with nothing else to do but fall into an amorous heap with Mrs. Rolston."

☆ ☆ ☆

Holmes had passed fifteen minutes discussing the situation with Mary and old Randolph, but then he had tired of the game. He was waiting for Klein. It was not that Holmes himself was incapable of drafting a memo, real or otherwise; there was, in any case, nothing in Klein's original article which had not struck him as either obviously right or naively wrong. Had it come around as a staff study, he'd probably have killed it by a "questionable" or "of dubious value." But had Klein's article not appeared at all, he might well have let the longer-range aspects go by the boards. In any case, the initiative had passed out of his hands. The result, he knew, was a dependence on Klein not unaccompanied by hostility.

Now Holmes briefed Klein on what had taken place at the NSC

meeting—"A depressing performance by all of us." Then he added, "On the brighter side, the Secretary did make a case for a longer-range, non-military solution, which could, if liberally translated, constitute a mandate for your conference."

Klein shrugged.

Holmes stared at him for an instant. "I think the first thing we should attend to . . ."

Now they're interested, Klein thought, though it seemed less important to him now. That was the way it always happened. As soon as he got what he wanted, his desire for it receded. He had been so bitter at Catherine, that she didn't keep up the house, that she shunned the sociability he so "gloried" in, as she put it, and, more importantly, or, so he had thought at the time, that she had refused to give him a child. But when she had finally agreed to it, had improved in other ways—he had to admit it—*then* he had threatened divorce.

Holmes was still talking. Klein nodded agreement to a point he had only half heard.

"The problem with those tactical nukes," Alex Gamarekian said in his chalk-talk voice, "is that they're being carried along, but they're not being used."

"Okay." Smith waited for his aide's guileless military logic.

"First of all, those weapons are not that mobile. If we have to retreat fast, it's going to be pretty frustrating dragging them around, especially if we're being clobbered."

"So what are you getting at?"

"I think he has a point," Franklin Harrison cut in. "He means, if you've got it, why not use it? Am I right?"

"It would look pretty silly on the Hill," Gamarekian said, "if our units start taking it, and they just have to sit there holding their dicks in their hands."

"Alex," Smith asked, "what's the alternative, though I suppose I can guess?"

"It's obvious: use the weapons right away. Why wait ten days to two weeks? They might not stop the Chinese for a while, but they could sure cut the shit out of 'em. And most important, they might protect our troops from being overrun. And they could also convince those gooks, right from the start, that we mean business!"

"Good, Alex," Smith said.

"So the President," Harrison cut back in, "will have no political alternative but to authorize them."

"Then we can assume," Smith concluded, "that the Joint Chiefs or Defense will ask the President for authorization to use the weapons right away. But the funny thing about it all is that, now that we know, there's not a damn thing we can do about it."

"Not a thing," Gamarekian agreed.

As Holmes descended into his lowest period, right after lunch, he believed in none of it, neither the war nor any other aspect of the game. His glasses were irritating the bridge of his nose. Klein's memo was pushy and overly academic. There he was, still sitting in Holmes's office with the same smug look on his face. "How can we possibly propose a general conference," Holmes asked him now, "while the Chinese are occupying a part of Thailand?"

"As I said on page three," Klein answered, "we'll get it because we'll reach a military stalemate, and then a conference will be the only means of settling it up."

Holmes smiled. "Do you think, Klein, we'll end up using those weapons?"

"Yes, I do *now*. I was thinking about it, and now I do."

Holmes had no ideas at all; the torpor inside his head was as total as the inside of a cinder block. He had to get started. Klein was sitting there no doubt impressed with himself, like a biology student dissecting his first frog.

"I can't see any other way now," Klein continued. "We could have had a conference without all this if we'd acted a few months ago."

"I presume you're speaking about your article?"

"Well, yes, in a way, because now we'll have to employ tactical weapons to knock the Chinese out, or at least stop them. But if we do, at the same time—and this is vitally important—we'll have to effect a full-scale intimidation to prevent them from using their missiles on *us*. The President will have to place our entire strategic force on alert, and make that clear to the Chinese; put SAC in the air and disperse it to civilian air bases; put Minuteman and MX on immediate countdown; station Polaris and Poseidons off the Chinese coast."

Klein was incredible!

"Do you want to go on with this deal, or not?" Klein demanded.

Holmes looked at him over the top of his glasses and said nothing. But before Klein had left, Holmes had paid his price by agreeing to ask the Secretary to invite him to the next NSC meeting.

☆ ☆ ☆

Smith stood up right in the middle of a session with his staff. "I'm getting out of here. I'm going to take ten." He headed down the corridor, nodding to "Tom," "Ambassador Harriman," "Mr. Coolidge," in a toneless voice, as if from a list.

Between the old and the new sections of the building, he traversed a glass-enclosed passageway that looked out over a parking lot to Virginia Avenue. Rat-tat-tat-tat—machine-gun bullets ripped through the glass. As he lay in a pool of his own blood, the sun shone in; traffic moved ceaselessly down the Avenue.

He dropped a dime in a public phone. "Hi, Sally."

"How's your day going?"

"Terrible."

"How come?"

"Oh, I don't know. The work, I suppose."

"Do you have time to talk?" she asked him.

"No."

"Well, even if you don't, you took it, so . . . I'm glad you called, because I was wondering whether or not to go to the hairdresser and sit under the great iron-head, or wait just a little longer for the big man's call."

"Yes, the big man."

" Do you know what I dreamt about last night?"

"No, Sally, I don't . . ."

"Shhh. It's got to do with the *game*, Zach. Well, I dreamt I was talking to Mao, you know, the one from China, and he was sitting on top of a wall, big and round, like Humpty-Dumpty, and I was wondering if he was going to fall, but he didn't wonder at all, not Mr. Mao, he just sat on the wall with a big grin on his face."

"You didn't dream that."

" 'Course not. I'll tell you what. I'll come down and meet you at the Madison for a down-the-hatch martini, and then a dinner. Hell, if Kennedy could swim in his pool with you know who, you ought to at least rate a martini; besides you're sexier than he *ever* was. What do you think of that?"

"You're marvelous!"

"I'll hang around like the CIA waiting for your call."

"If I can't make it, you'll know it's not because I didn't try, or didn't want to, or don't love you, Sally Jenks."

"Good-bye, darling. I know you've got to go."

"I do. I'll call. Goodbye." Back in his office, he dictated a memo to Henderson. Did it take into account all the main points he'd wanted to make in the meeting?

White: World Monitoring Service, Peking, December 7, 1500 Hours, Flash Transcription

OFFICIAL USE ONLY

Joint Communique of Shih-Ying Chen, Acting Chairman of the Central Committee of the People's Republic of China, and A. G.

Kuznetsov, Foreign Minister of the Union of Soviet Socialist Republics

Messrs. Chen and Kuznetsov discussed in comradely fashion the situation in Southeast Asia and, in particular, the imperialist aggression of the United States and its puppet allies. The statesmen pledged the untiring efforts of the two leading socialist countries to thwart efforts by the United States to colonize the peoples of the region, and agreed that this topic should be taken up again at the earliest possible opportunity.

"Well, you've seen the communiqué," Henderson said to the Secretary of State as they waited for the NSC meeting to begin. "I think it's clear enough *now* how things sit between the Chinese and Soviets."

"How?" Vane asked mildly.

"Well, I should think it's obvious that the Soviets have given the Chinese the go-ahead."

"It seemed a relatively innocuous document to me."

"Really. Isn't it apparent the Soviets are on board? I think the sooner we present an ultimatum with those tactical nukes, the better. I'd be for doing it right now!"

"It occurs to me," said the Secretary, "that here we have a good occasion to practice a less showy, less bellicose mode of diplomacy than we have in the past. I shall attempt to delay as much as I can any ultimatum, as you put it."

"I couldn't disagree more."

"You will, I trust, confine your disagreement to the Departmental staff, for I mean to insist strongly on what I have just said, and I do not contemplate any disagreement in my Department appearing at the meeting."

Henderson said nothing.

Smith looked the other way, and then moved off to talk to Wally

Perkins, who had just arrived. To Perkins, of course, he mentioned nothing of what he had just heard.

"This meeting," the Secretary said, after he had seated himself at the head of the table, "takes place in the light of continual advances of Chinese arms. Mr. Mikesell, our understanding is that you would produce a report. We don't have much time."

"This morning," Mikesell began, "some doubt was expressed about the use of tactical nuclear weapons in Thailand."

"Yes, some doubt," Vane snapped.

"Our studies now indicate," the Secretary of Defense continued, "that unless we can authorize our units in Northern and Central Thailand to employ tactical nuclear weapons, they are likely to be overrun."

Vane cut him off. "But, as we discussed, with the troops we have, even if you used those weapons, we couldn't hold the ground. The tactic now is to buy time."

Mikesell gestured him away with a sweep of his hand. "Mr. Secretary, it is clear that the only adequate means of defense is tactical nuclear weapons. Accordingly, I called the President and suggested to him that we tell the Communists that nuclear weapons *will* be used unless they desist, and if they do not desist, the weapons will be used immediately."

"You called the President to tell him *that*!" Vane actually looked rattled. "Did he agree, did he agree to something as foolish as an ultimatum?"

A Control officer appeared, walked quietly up to the television screen, and switched it on. The President was standing before a podium, apparently at the White House; there were the twin flags, the oval curve of the press room. The President was saying, "The Chinese Communists should make no mistake. The United States does not propose to sit back and watch them brazenly take over Thailand. Effective five p.m. today, I, Mitchell Murray, President of the United States, have given my authorization to American units in the field to employ tactical nuclear weapons, if necessary, to stop the Communist advance."

Vane muttered, "Did the President say . . . did he agree to *that*?"

"In forty-eight hours, if the Communists do not halt their attack in Thailand, the weapons will be used."

"He said he would wait, that we would discuss this! We had an agreement!"

The President continued. "The Chinese Communists have threatened to use nuclear weapons themselves, and have even threatened to retaliate against American cities. The United States does not intend to submit to such threats. The Communist nuclear force is only a small fraction of the nuclear force of the United States. But as a precaution, I have placed the Strategic Air Command, the Ballistic Missile System, and other elements of our retaliatory force on full alert.

"Only the most wanton disregard for the lives of their own people—farmers, school teachers, factory workers, people just like yourselves—could permit the Communists to ignore these preparations.

"We do not wish to threaten or to humiliate the young new rulers of China; we wish only to put an end to aggression. We regret having to use the weapons of war, and would much prefer to practice the arts of peace. If the Communists wish to sit down and negotiate our differences, the United States is ready right now.

"But let me make one thing unmistakably clear. The territory of Thailand, or that of any other free people, is not negotiable. The independence of a free people cannot be an object at the bargaining table. The Communists must, as a symbol of good faith, withdraw all their troops from Thailand.

"Once that is done, the United States will be willing to participate in a conference of all countries in Southeast Asia, and all other countries which might have an interest there, to seek a path to peace. The path to peace is open; now it is up to the Communist to take it."

The Control officer turned off the set.

"Well, that's it," Smith said. "He's given them the ultimatum. He's done it!"

Holmes visualized a solid sheet of white paint, with one edge of red or orange. Behind that were edges of still other colors; then there was neither white, nor colors, nor even black, but nothing, which was the non-meeting. For just a moment, he had been there.

It's just a game, Smith said to himself, just a silly game. But if that was all it was, why was he so excited? Did those people realize what a five-megaton bomb could do? Just one?

As Sansone waited for the Secretary to end the meeting, he had the sense of his body like a sick pigeon with a swollen, translucent head. It was so large it filled the entire room!

The Secretary concluded the meeting by announcing that the State Department would be preparing contingency plans for handling the "longer-range aspects of problem, as requested by the President." Only the slightest unevenness in his delivery gave a sign of how discouraged he must be. Holmes would have comforted him; held, if only metaphorically, the Secretary's head in his arms, soothed his forehead with his palm. But Vane would have had none of it. He'd have sprung out at him like a switchblade. Now he said, "Frank, Allen, Zach, Stoddard, yes, and Michael, I'd like you to come to my office at, say, ten to four."

The Secretary began the meeting by describing the telephone conference he'd just had with the President and the Secretary of Defense. "Apparently some time after our meeting this morning, the President decided to go ahead with the nuclear threat, and prepared the statement you've just heard. This was, of course, contrary to the assurances given me by the Secretary of Defense, although I have no doubt, none at all, that Mr. Mikesell was operating in good faith. There was also apparently considerable pressure on the President, particularly a call from the Senate Majority Leader, to which he had to respond.

"In any case, the President maintained that he could be most effective by making our position clear immediately, by taking a strong position *now* rather than by probing the Communists over the next few weeks. He apparently felt that if the Communists seriously wanted to negotiate, this tactic would in no way jeopardize that opportunity. So, as I say, he went ahead. But I am far from discouraged by the final result. The threat of nuclear weapons was much toned down—and, although a forty-eight hour limit is still on, there is more of a chance now that we can avoid using those weapons. And I am sure you will see in the discussion of a conference much of our thinking."

Holmes observed with admiration the tilt of Vane's chin, his clear gaze.

Sansone smiled to himself. So the Secretary had been double-crossed. Even so, he was not accusing Mikesell, not by so much as a word. He was a pro. No doubt about it!

Smith rubbed his lips with his thumb, as if to wipe away the bad taste.

Now the situation was set, Klein thought, where his memo would have to be discussed. But when the Secretary finally did turn to his conference, he didn't seem to care. Holmes seemed to notice it, too, as perhaps did the others. The Secretary seemed to be receding behind his own voice. Klein saw his conference disappear like the headlights of a car down a darkened street.

"As for the countries which might attend," Vane was saying, "it would hardly seem our task to decide which ones have interests in the area and which have not."

"I suppose we'll fight that out with our cosponsors," Henderson put it.

"Yes, we might. And then you have the problem of location," the Secretary added. "I can imagine it in some dreary neutral haven, the rain seeping in through the stucco."

For a moment Holmes might have interposed himself, but it was doubtful if he had any more enthusiasm for the project now than had the Secretary. What one needed, he thought, was a driver, a Henderson—but Henderson, having gone too far this morning, had been subdued. And had Henderson seized the problem right now, his clutch would have felt like cold grease.

Sansone had not offered a comment. He knew now that the Secretary had had it, and that if they were to come up with anything, he must be the one to take it on. But he felt so lousy. He was just about to speak, when he could hear Anne telling him he should wait a day, rest awhile, or Christ, take a few months off. It would be good for him, instead of pushing, pushing all the time, so he'd come home like an old locomotive, shaking and coughing. But what a story he could tell, as he settled back with a drink and went through the whole day—it all seeming, even for him, to come out of his barrel chest, that magic barrel which was full of butterflies. He'd tell her how he'd rammed this through, or pushed that across, as his fatigue washed away in the flood and surging waters of his pride.

"Why don't we get a girl in here," Sansone said, "so we can whip up a final draft. There're a couple of things here everybody's agreed on. Let's nail them down right off. But first, what about cosponsors? What do you say to the U.S., U.S.S.R., and Communist China? I think right *there* we'd make a big point without giving up a whole lot in substance."

When the secretary came in, Holmes half expected her to be nude. Sansone's proposal *was* dramatic. And once they agreed to it, the meeting got going.

Klein said nothing. He felt like a woman being used by a man she doesn't like. It was not molestation, she was not being abused; only it gave her no pleasure, and him, apparently, a lot.

Good for you, Smith said to himself. Somebody needed to kick ass. But he said aloud, "I wonder if, after the fighting, anyone will want to do any talking."

"That's not at issue here," the Secretary said, and turned to the Senator to go on.

Led by Sansone, they worked it through, discussing, amending, joking, deferring to the Secretary, or simply agreeing, as Vane dictated the points to the secretary: the sponsors, the general organization of the conference, the declaration of principles, the economic secretariat, the prohibition on foreign troops, the limitation on advisers, the observer mechanism. One by one, they worked through the main headings of Klein's memo, until it became clear not only that they'd have something to show Defense, but that they actually *had* something.

Sansone wasn't so sure, but his job was to get it through, and he pushed ahead.

Holmes had maintained a bemused wonderment as Klein's memo was being pushed forward; he had never believed in it. Millennial excitement was hardly to be expected, except from Klein, who now must see his efforts crowning the age.

Smith felt like a member of a football team which, though still far behind, had just scored two touchdowns. But as the memo rounded out, there was still something he needed to ask. "It seems to me we've got to think about how we're going to *get* to this conference, how we're going to get the Soviets and the Chinese to come, much less cosponsor." It was ten to seven, ten minutes before he'd arranged to see Sally Jenks.

The Secretary sighed. "I'm not sure at all that the conference will actually happen. The President has proposed it, and, I suppose, the problem does remain how we shall make it attractive."

"All right," Smith persisted, "then just tell me this. What'll happen if we really start slugging it out in Thailand? It seems to me *then* we'll be less and less willing ourselves to negotiate unless we can say we're winning. What'll happen if we can't, if our casualties have started mounting and we're in serious trouble?"

"I wouldn't know," said the Secretary. "But, you'll forgive my cynicism, using nuclear weapons would make it easier for us, wouldn't it? The whole business . . . Well . . ."

"Hell, all we need now," Sansone said, "is what we've got right here!"

"Yes," the Secretary said. "We'll have it typed up, and then let's come back here in an hour and see what it looks like."

☆ ☆ ☆

BLACK: COMMANDER, U.S. FORCES THAILAND, DEC 8, 0542 HRS, FLASH SUMMARY (PASS TO PRESIDENT)

TOP SECRET

UNITS l2TH AND 23RD CHICOM ROUTE ARMIES STAGED NIGHT ASSAULTS US THAI POSITIONS DAN SAI AND BAN THA LI, BUT BROKE OFF. THEN SWEPT AROUND POSITIONS AND CUT THEM OFF. 2000 TO 2500 US AND 3500 TO 4000 THAI TROOPS TRAPPED WITH LITTLE CHANCE OF RESCUE.

DESPITE POUNDING US AIR FORCE, ENEMY CONTINUING ADVANCE AGAINST LITTLE OPPOSITION. WILL PROBABLY REACH OUTSKIRTS UDON THANI BEFORE EFFECTIVE RESISTANCE POSSIBLE, IF THEN.

☆ ☆ ☆

As Zach Smith left the building, the cold night air—the sky was a post-sunset purple—hit his legs, chest, and face with his longing for Sally Jenks. He cut through the parking lot and entered the Madison Hotel.

He was ten minutes late, but Sally hadn't even arrived. As he sat waiting in the lobby, it occurred to him that he had been arguing about a nonexistent event. But even as he'd argued, reality had crept in like wild animals around a dying campfire. Where was Sally Jenks? There was so little time!

Another twenty minute, Sally appeared. "Where were you?"

"I'm sorry I'm late." Sally looked harassed, the way she always did when she was late, which she always was.

"It's seven-thirty."

"I wanted to dress up for you, Zach, and I got started putting up my hair with combs. Do you like it? It got later than I thought. Have you ever seen a blond flamenco dancer?"

"No."

"Don't be mad, Zach. And you haven't seen my dress yet, because I just bought it, and when you do, how could you be mad, or you could be for just a little while, but not after a good drink, and a ten-minute, down-the-hatch, eight-course dinner. I'm sorry I'm late. Here, help me off with my coat, so you can see my dress."

It was red and low-cut. She stood waiting for his judgment, as if she would disrobe right there if he wanted her.

"You look nice."

"You're still angry."

"No, it's just late."

"Okay, but now let's have a drink. Let's just have a drink, and we'll talk, and eat a little, not a lot. I'll have something for you when you come home. And, Zach, look at me from time to time, just every so often peek at me over your angry brows, okay?"

"Okay." He smiled; he knew he was smiling. He signaled stiffly to the *maitre 'd*, and ordered for her a Galliano Stinger—it was one of Sally's drinks he'd never heard of before they met—and for himself a Manhattan, and some little sandwiches.

They sat saying nothing. She traced patterns with her red fingernail in the dew of her glass; he glanced at her from time to time over his "angry brows."

"You're tired."

"I was in meetings all day, and I've got to be back at eight."

"Did you believe me when I told you I dreamt about Mao?"

"No."

"I could have. I believe in dreams in a funny way."

"Why?"

"Because they can be true, Zach."

"But they aren't. You were making the whole thing up."

"Well, if I could have made it up, I could have dreamt it, too, because I would have had a reason. And when things have a reason, then I believe in them, so *that*, Zachariah Smith, is why I believe in dreams." She smiled, but only a little. "You weren't listening," she said.

"I did listen, but it didn't help, not about dreams. If I'm going to believe in something, it's got to be true."

"Even dreams that *mean* something to you?"

"Okay."

"Do you really see?"

"I think so," Smith said.

"Have a sandwich. I'll pick it out for you and charm it into a roast beef *au jus.*"

"Thank you, darling."

"You practically took my finger off, you bastard!"

"Not so loud!" They sat for a minute in silence, and then he said, "The Security Council's at eight, and I don't have an idea yet what the Soviets are going to do."

☆ ☆ ☆

Michael Klein had called Catherine as soon as he'd checked back with his office. She'd fixed him shrimp creole, which he always said he liked, but she should have known he'd probably have to stay down tonight. "I'll heat it up again when you come home, but it won't be the same."

"You act like it's my fault I have to stay here; I'd like to be home, too."

But he knew that all the advantages were his. His "smug little isle," she called his office. Now she said, "I went to all the trouble to fix it, and you don't seem to care. You always say I don't do things for you, and when I do, it doesn't seem to matter."

"Of course it does."

A big flag was slowly flapping in the wind as a horse ran around a racetrack lined with palm trees, an exhausted horse, its hooves pounding, like its heart. Michael said, "I'm sorry I was cross. You were a dear to fix the shrimp. You and Helen have it now, but sit with me anyway when I come home. Do you have a wine? I can bring a nice Sauterne."

"That was part of the treat."

"You *are* a dear!"

"It's a good one."

"You really are."

What an unctuous dialogue, he thought, and then said, "You wonder whether things like that aren't the only things that finally make any difference. I mean the accretion of such acts."

"You always have to erect everything into a principle."

"Well, isn't it true?"

"I'm not mocking you, Michael. It's just so characteristic. You're talking about *little acts of kindness*, I suppose. I'm not sure they aren't all swept away in some larger set of events. If you have a hurricane, or you have a war and your country's bombed, and everything's destroyed, what difference do they make?"

Sansone had gone over to the Castlereagh with his aides Tucker McGrath and Wylie Adams. On the way, they picked up Wally Perkins, who still managed to look like a reporter of the early forties.

"That's one amazing hat you're wearing," Sansone said. "They don't make fedoras like that anymore, not with such a high crown. I always wondered where you got it."

"You've probably seen quite a few of them by now. I've worn the same shape ever since I came to this town, and that's before the war, Frank. I get 'em from Margolis & Sons. The old man's been dead for years, but they still make 'em up for me the same way."

"Marvelous!"

"Sort of a little bell tower up there," Adams snickered.

Perkins said, "People got to know me by my hat."

"I remember," Sansone said, "when you were wearing a metal pot in the war. I used to look for your column, 'On the Line,' in *Stars and Stripes*."

"You got a good memory, Frank."

"It was a good column. I confess that occasionally, after reading it, if the supply was short, I might find another purpose for it, with all due respect."

"Glad to be of help." Perkins stared away. "Did you know I never left the States? Most of that column, Frank, was made up."

"Huh, you could have fooled me. I spent my forty-first birthday in a foxhole in Tarawa."

"Swatting mosquitoes?"

"Real mosquitoes." Sansone shook his head. "How did I end up playing this game?"

"It's the luck of the draw, I guess."

"You've got to end up somewhere." He picked up the menu. "We'd better order, if we're ever going to get it down."

Holmes had a tray brought up to his office. When he'd been forced to work long hours, it had always been his pleasure to eat alone. He now sat imagining a Sung scroll that hung in a corner behind the desk in his study at home. It depicted a group of foot soldiers on their way to the front. Simple peasants, hot, a little disheveled, probably swearing or telling stories of their villages or wives as they marched. War was part of life, a calamity, to be sure, but a calamity still under the dome of heaven. And if one were a gentleman, like Holmes himself, one accepted war, indeed all things in a calm, determined manner: the morality of a great culture with a long frontier and continual wars.

He thought of the three plums, one hardly a suggestion of an outline, that hung against the other wall. It was the acceptance of the plums, he thought, which called them forth from the wall, else they receded into nothingness.

His buzzer went off. He gave a start.

☆ ☆ ☆

BLUE: US MISSION UN, DEC 7, 1742 HRS

OFFICIAL USE ONLY

INITIAL REACTIONS PRESIDENT'S SPEECH GENERALLY FAVORABLE, THO SOME DELS DISTURBED POSSIBILITY USE ATOMIC WEAPONS. NADAR (INDIA) WAS FEARFUL 48 HOUR LIMIT WOULD LOOK TOO MUCH TO CHINESE LIKE ULTIMATUM AND MAKE NEGOTIATIONS MORE DIFFICULT. HE PRAISED QTE OTHERWISE CONSTRUCTIVE TONE UNQTE OF SPEECH. MICKIEWIEZ (POLAND) SAID SPEECH WOULD FORCE CHICOMS TO BRINK AND THAT US MOVE OPENED POSSIBILITY OF NUCLEAR WAR TO MAINTAIN QTE US SPHERE OF INFLUENCE UNQTE. . .

KIRKLAND

☆ ☆ ☆

BLUE: US MISSION UN, DEC 7, 1852 HRS

SECRET

MICHAUX (BELGIUM) SHOWED ME DRAFT RESOLUTION, CONTAINED SEPTEL, WHICH CONDEMNS CHINESE AGGRESSION IN THAILAND AND OTHERWISE PARALLELS OUR THINKING. IN VIEW PRESIDENT'S SPEECH, I SUGGESTED FINAL ADDITIONAL PARAGRAPH WHICH QTE CALLS UPON ALL NATIONS IN THE AREA AND ALL OTHER NATIONS WITH SUBSTANTIAL INTERESTS THERE TO CONVENE AN INTERNATIONAL CONFERENCE, UNDER UNITED NATIONS AUSPICES, TO

DISCUSS SECURITY ARRANGEMENTS AND PROBLEMS OF
COMMON CONCERN. UNQTE.

KIRKLAND

The State Department team assembled once again in the Secretary's office and read through the text of their memo. Everyone was ready to sign on except Smith. "I still think," he said, "that we ought to have something in here about how we're going to get to this conference."

He looked to Henderson, but Henderson was doodling flags on his notepad, a ghostly little United Nations to distract himself. Smith shrugged. "I hope it works."

Maybe he was right, but Holmes said nothing. After all, some piece of paper had to get out. At ten to nine, did Smith ask him to *believe* in this conference, as an event which would take place on this earth, with delegates, translators, felt-covered tables? Enough that they had thought of it at all, or that, miraculously, it had become a Departmental memo. Smith expected too much. Well, time enough tomorrow. Holmes gathered up his papers.

As Sansone reviewed Kirkland's speech, he discovered that the UN session was being broadcast on educational TV. There was the Security Council table with national delegations seated around it, and there was what appeared to be a Thai diplomat just starting his speech. Amazing! Sansone lit a cigarette and settled back to listen.

"It was a pretty grim speech," Wylie said, when they'd heard it out. "I can't say I would blame them, faced with the end of their national existence."

"What a crazy-ass business," Sansone said. "Sitting up late at night listening to somebody go on like that, when it's all a fake. When I was running for office in Newark, I always used to make a pitch to the national heroes: Emmet, O'Connell, say, if I was in an Irish district, or Garibaldi, names like that, for us. I wonder if their country means as much to the Thais. Well, maybe it does. Just because they're little and brown and far away. Christ, what do I know?"

"If this was a jury trial," Tucker said, "the UN would order the Chinese out and make them pay damages. The 'Court of World Opinion.'"

He started to laugh at his own joke, but Sansone waved him quiet. Kirkland was next, and then Federov.

At Dupont Circle, there was an old Negro who sold flowers until late into the evening. How many would rot before they were sold, Klein thought. And still the man demanded $4.75 a bunch. Under the streetlight, the big, dark honeyed mums recessed into malice—*fleurs du mal.* The wizened Negro moved like a gypsy in the shadows, clipping their stems, wrapping them up in newspaper.

"Do you sell many this time of night?"

The flower seller looked at Klein as if he were stamping the back of Klein's hand with an ultraviolet sign. "I just sold you a bunch," he said. Klein hurriedly paid him.

Klein's daughter, Helen, was at the door. In her hand, she carried an edition of Schubert lieder. "Hello, Dad."

She had her mother's eyes, as if they were staring at him through a mask. How could he have a seventeen year-old daughter? Except for her, everything in the world, his life with Catherine, his teaching, his sense of his own progress in life, had seemed to stop. Only Helen seemed to grow in those years.

She would be the accompanist at a recital at the Academy next Saturday. She said she didn't have any problem with the lieder technically. She just didn't feel any emotion.

When Klein was a boy her age, he'd had a vision of his older sister. It was just a few months before she died; she was bedridden, and already pale with leukemia. It had been in the winter, by a frozen fountain in the park. Although his sister Helen had not been there, he'd actually seen her skating. She was in a short skirt and black tights, and was making intricate circles on the ice.

☆ ☆ ☆

"My dear," Holmes turned to Mary Watts, "may I offer you my cab?"

"I should have liked that, but just a few minutes ago, in anticipation of our release, I called my husband. I'm afraid the poor man has already left."

Holmes put on his coat, took up his Homburg and umbrella. At the C Street entrance he found a waiting cab. As it sped away, *the road to Moscow now lay open before him.* Was that a line from *War and Peace*? He conjured up a picture of Napoleon sitting tight-lipped in a coach, then of the emperor's maps and toilet kit, the one of silver and red felt he'd seen in Paris at the Carnavalet Museum. Like a capsule, weightless and quiet, the cab seemed to project him into the night.

☆ ☆ ☆

When Smith left the meeting, he took with him an Irish elf. "I'll be back," the elf protested, as if he were being hauled out of a bar. Outside, the elf said to the stars, "Twinkle, twinkle," like a charwoman grumbling to herself after the lady of the house had left. "What a lot of nonsense, plain nonsense, I call it!"

What could Smith say? "You're probably right," he laughed good-humoredly. Smith's good humor was hard to resist. "You make me sick," answered the elf.

"What do you *want* me to say?" Smith asked.

"That's your worry," said the elf. Smith would say nothing. He was going home, he'd had enough for one day; and beyond it, as if over a wall, or across the sea, was Sally Jenks, where now he must sink or swim as if the rest of the world did not exist. "Sally Jenks," he said to her on his imaginary car radio, "this is J. Zachariah Smith."

He pulled up in front of his house in Bethesda. Somewhere, while he was driving, it had struck him that Sally Jenks had come all the way into town just to have dinner with him, or a drink, as it turned out. Didn't it demean her to come in like that, just for him?

He kissed her quickly at the door. "I've got to watch television— they're putting on the game. Could you bring my dinner in here?" Sally just stood there. "Do you know that in Thailand it's ten o'clock in the morning, and that the Chinese are supposed to be beating our brains out?"

Sally squinted. "Before dinner, I think we ought to have a little drink, just to get to know one another better. I always say I don't know a man I haven't had a drink with. Yes, sir, what'll it be, Mr. Smith, a little Jack Daniels on the rocks?"

"I just want dinner, Sally."

"I thought my name was Sally Jenks."

"What difference does it make? I don't want a drink. I just want to eat, and watch the goddamn television, and go to sleep. I'm exhausted!"

"I'm just as tired as you are because I didn't do a goddamn thing all day!"

"Should I get the dinner myself?"

"Yeah, go get it yourself, J. Zachariah Smith! Go fuck yourself, too, J. Zachariah Smith!" She slammed the door.

Klein leaned back in his chair. "It was a wonderful meal!" he exclaimed. "A triumph!"

"Helen contributed the *mousse*," Catherine put in.

"It was marvelous, a *tour de force!*"

"Oh, Daddy, it was just plain *mousse*."

"You make it sound like straw, you child of privilege."

"Mama said you wanted something nice. And here, I've done it, and all I get is a lecture on my advantages under the class system. After the revolution, you'd be the first to go."

"For my last meal, I'll order shrimp creole and *mousse*."

"And then off with his head," Catherine cried.

"And we'll march him to the wall," Helen sang, "briefs, textbooks and all. And he'll cry, 'Perhaps a little *mousse* to fill my maw, before I lose my head.' And that will be all, as his head rolls into the straw, along with his briefs, textbooks and all."

There was nothing more *he* could do; they were using his memo point-for-point, even if the idea was supposed to be Sansone's, even if . . .

"Did you like it? his daughter asked.

"What?"

"My song."

"Of course." Hadn't he told her? "Do you want to talk now about the lieder?"

"Okay." Helen waited for him.

"Well, my idea is that if you know what the lyrics mean, it might be easier to play the songs."

She said nothing.

"Do you know what they mean?"

She shook her head.

"You could be thinking about them when you play."

Helen shrugged, but followed him over to the piano. There was still nothing in her face, but, with Catherine there, he translated the Goethe, Schiller, Heine, and Ossian from the German, as Helen played. He spoke in a quiet, plain voice, leaving the emotions to her, till well past midnight.

Maybe something had happened; you couldn't tell. He kissed his daughter goodnight. Then he made love to his wife, as if moonlight were shining on water. Was that a line from Ossian?

☆ ☆ ☆

Holmes's plunge into domesticity was relieved by Betty's new coat. It was Navy blue in the baronet style, with a brave front of gold buttons across the chest. It wasn't altogether bad, although Betty's chunky figure was hardly fitting for the severe new line.

"It's magnificent," he assured her.

Her blue eyes anxiously sought his. "Do you really think so? I bought it from my favorite saleslady at Bonwit's. I've had such luck with her; she's never let me down, at least that I can remember, well, maybe once. And I thought it would be so nice to have it tonight for the Wildes' party." Her eyes went wide. "Oh dear, we *are* going to the Wildes', aren't we? You must be exhausted, and here I am dragging you to a party."

"We shall go," he said. "I shouldn't miss the opportunity of escorting you in your new coat for all the tea in . . . Ah, I wonder what the Chinese are up to, as it were."

"I would like to go not merely to exhibit myself—I hope you're being sincere in saying you like the coat—but because Florence Wilde is such a curious person. She's just published her sixth novel, I think it's her sixth. And finally, I know I'm sounding like a lawyer, but anyway, you seem to thrive on sociability like Napoleon on his baths."

"We shall go, by all means!" Holmes exclaimed.

"Good."

"I was just thinking about Napoleon myself as I was riding home in the cab." On the television, the Soviet representative was going on at tedious length. "His mind was curiously compartmentalized. I feel a bit like him."

"You are like him in that way."

"I lack juice, no doubt: that's the deficiency. I'm a prune to his plum, yes? But on the other side, I lack his *gaucherie*."

"Are you listening to the television? We'll be late as it is!"

"I am listening," he insisted. "Did my thoughts about Napoleon distress you? You were the one who brought him up. But that's not fair, is it? Let me hear the Chinese, and then we shall be off to the

Wildes. Your coat, my dear, is a triumph, if somewhat ill-fitting in the back."

Smith sat with a drink in front of his television set, waiting to hear Ambassador Federov with a pad of paper and a certain quantity of dread. "You're on," Smith said. Anything that made him feel that way must be real, in some sense, at least. He listened for the clue that would tell him the Soviets had a deal on with the Chinese—the shade of intimacy, the extra confidence which would give it away. But nothing came. To be sure, it was a tough speech. He had expected that, but the Soviets really *did* seem detached.

Events in Thailand, Federov said, should finally have taught the American militarists the full folly of their policy. But their threat to use nuclear weapons could only embitter the conflict. Only madmen would resort to such weapons when peaceful means of settlement lay ready at hand. That was it?

Smith dialed his office, and got Franklin Harrison—his aide was still there. "This is Zach. Unless I'm wrong, there's no deal on with the Chinese!"

"You're fast," Harrison said.

"I think we can define the Soviets' interests as one, to reduce American military influence in the area, and two, to keep the Chinese out. Do you agree?"

"Almost," Harrison said. "How much do they want in themselves?"

"That's my next point," Smith answered. "I think now they're looking for a mediating role, a senior-statesman stance. That communiqué with the Chinese was just window dressing. They're not involved, and they're willing now to settle for prestige. Well, what I want to do is draft a presidential letter to Chairman Rogachev suggesting that the Russians actually mediate. We can work up something tonight, and then we'll get it right to the Secretary. I'll drive down and be there in twenty minutes. By that time, you can have checked out the Chinese speech."

"Do you really want to go on with this?" Harrison asked. "It's past eleven, and Alex and I were just . . ."

"I said I'll be there in twenty minutes!"

Sansone listened intently to the speeches coming from the make-believe UN. Communist China was the country he wanted to hear, but when their representative finally started to speak, it was all propaganda: "militaristic cliques," "stooges of the capitalists," "vanguard of history." What the hell was he talking about? What about the atomic business? Intermittently, Sansone looked up at the clock—the minute hand seemed to be crawling around the face of the dial.

Finally, the Chinese representative got around to the President's speech. "The Chinese people will not be threatened by a country which has given up any pretense of moral decency." That stung a little, but what were they prepared to do about it? Yes, yes, they were armed with "nuclear weapons of the most advanced type," which was bullshit, but were they prepared to use them? And then, "If the American President chooses to use nuclear weapons, he must be prepared for whatever consequences will follow."

Christ! He had waited up three hours for *that*! Nothing! It was already past eleven. He headed out the office.

On the corridor walls were valentine lace doilies with flowers and red hearts, and beneath chest level, white marble facing like at Russo & Sons Undertakers, everything smeared with a thin layer of translucent wax. The pinwheels of white revolved, the flowers sucked, the marble lustered.

He stood at the family grave site, the plots at a strange tilt. Beneath him was the grave of his brother, Giorgio, with its American flag and plastic flowers. *Died July 8, 1944, at Saint-Lô, France.*

As he descended in the elevator, a young man said to him, "Quite a day, sir." Sansone nodded, unsure whether to be grateful or irritated. "Quite a day," he said, but soundlessly, as if his voice were paralyzed. He nodded again to the young man, then looked away. He leaned against the elevator; the drive in the night air would do him good.

He found his car; adjusted the key, the heat, the headlights, the automatic window. The car started to roll out from the lot as if he were not driving it. As it turned into Virginia Avenue, faces were with him, spirits, people he knew, riding his tailpipe.

"Okay," he said. He'd tell his daughter, Gilda, he'd been on a 'trip,' but without whatever it was kids took nowadays. The spirits were still unshakeably there. His Buick, as it glided by the river, was like a broomstick. Here and there he caught the gleam of moonlight on the water, while underneath the river flowed and, on the other side he could see the dark hills of Virginia. He swooped under the overpasses as if pursued by pipes and flutes, only to emerge every few seconds into flowing transcripts of time. He felt his forehead. It was wet, but as the car gained Wisconsin Avenue, the periods of calm were lengthening out. He'd be fine. He hadn't been afraid, or only a little.

"Gilda, get your old man a ginger-ale," he said to his daughter, who was still up. "Ginger jail," she used to call it when she was a little girl. (Giorgio, Paula, Peter, Joe, Teresa were already gone.) My God, how beautiful she was. He didn't approve of the clothes she wore— the holes in her jeans, as if they couldn't afford decent clothes, the short skirts past her ears like a whore on a street corner. He'd talked to her about that. And she was already on the pill, although she wasn't really doing anything, was she? If she wasn't, why was she on the goddamn pill? Anne insisted she wasn't, that it was just a precaution. Were they all putting something over on him, because if he ever caught her, he'd . . . Pains shot through his chest.

"Thanks," he said, when she reappeared. "They were putting the game on television, the game I'm playing at the State Department— did you watch?"

"Mom told me. But it's all boring speeches, isn't it? I mean, politicians don't really say what they mean in speeches, right?"

"I thought you might be interested."

"That's what you've always said yourself."

"So you got that piece of worldly wisdom from me?"

"Well, I've listened before, I mean to the real one. We had to at school. It just sounded like guck." She went off to bed.

As Smith drove into the Department from Bethesda, he plugged in his Dictaphone and started in.

"To: The President

"From: The Secretary of State

"Subject: Draft Letter for Your Signature to Chairman Rogachev on Southeast Asia

"Dear Chairman Rogachev . . ." Smith went on dictating as he glided along upper Wisconsin Avenue on the long drop to the Potomac. *"I would propose that this conference be chaired by the Soviet Union, the People's Republic of China, and by the United States."* At a stoplight, he pulled up much too close to another car. He'd have to be careful. *"In order to effect a peace, and to help create an atmosphere of mutual accommodation, the United States is prepared now to make a number of significant concessions. The first would be our pledge to cease all military flights from bases in Thailand into Viet Nam, Laos, and Cambodia. The second . . ."*

Seventeen minutes later, he flipped the machine off. With the exception of a near crackup, he'd noticed absolutely nothing, as if his car had been on automatic pilot. He pressed the copy button and listened wistfully to the clack and hum as sheets of paper slowly emerged from a plastic slit. The machine sat on the seat adjoining him in a little halter like that used for an infant.

When Betty and Stoddard Holmes arrived at the Wildes, the

party was at full pitch, like a pulsating hive. The queen was Florence Wilde, whose novels, Holmes had heard, were written by a New York syndicate.

Her husband's money was said to be in real estate and submerged securities. He'd never been known to put in an appearance at one of these affairs; indeed, now that he thought of it, Holmes began to doubt the man's existence. He could imagine Wilde, though, like a bee on his one night, flying high above the Potomac, with the Capitol glittering like jewels below. His wings would be vibrating to invisibility as he impregnated his wife with his vast, socially potent wealth, only to descend drained and lethargic to . . . But what other purpose did he have?

Florence Wilde always dressed with extravagance, tonight in a wire mesh over a body stocking. Her glasses were of the new two-toned variety which oddly deflected light and gave the wearer a certain air of obliqueness or indirection. But the angles, so far as Holmes could see, converged on vacuity. He paid his entrance fee of quips and compliments; then he and Betty drifted into the crowd.

Holmes noted, as would everyone else, all the notables Florence Wilde had managed to assemble, three of these and several of those, and the ambassadors to this or that, as if in a game-bag. He thought, as he threaded his way to the drinks, of that riposte of Kennedy to the American Nobel Prize winners: that they had constituted the greatest collection of talent ever assembled in the White House, with the possible exception of when Thomas Jefferson had dined alone. At the drinks table, Holmes found Morris Friedlander. He raised his glass, and gave him a weak smile.

"We both should be writhing with guilt," Friedlander said. "Dallying here in the midst of this grave international crisis." His eyes scanned the crowd; in his hand was a second drink.

"Not at all," Holmes replied. "All this *sociabilitá* does us a world of good. Tomorrow morning the Chinese will find us alive and responsive, due precisely to tonight's harmless dissipations."

A tall, well-built young brunette sidled up to Friedlander—in a dress, Holmes noted, which was cut low in the back to the breach of decency. "Evelyn Winters, Stoddard Holmes. Stoddard takes care of all our Asiatic friends, and maybe our enemies, too, in that game I was telling you about."

"How interesting." Evelyn wore an Empire wig and moth-like lashes. Fetching, would have been Betty's word for her, if she'd liked her; crude, if she hadn't. Yes, crude would be more likely.

"Stoddard's harmless. He doesn't take *anything* too seriously."

"Did you know," Holmes told Evelyn, "that Morris lives at the White House these days, that his Georgetown address is a mere front."

"Is that why I see so little of you?" She looked into Friedlander's eyes with the disappointment of having wasted several years sleeping with the wrong man. Had Mitchell Murray carried Illinois and California, Friedlander might *in fact* have headed the National Security Council. "Is that true, Morris? Has the President confined you to quarters?"

"It's devotion, Evelyn." Friedlander turned abruptly to Holmes. "You should know, Stoddard, that the President and I had a go-around on your memo just before I left. Frankly, the President"—he glanced at Evelyn—"felt it gave away too much. He's worried that the whole business might play out on the Hill or in the press like an Asiatic Munich."

"Murray's faith is refreshing. To think that the public even remembers Munich!"

"You know this whole game is being played in a fishbowl. I think it's come home to Murray that, real or not, his prestige is seriously involved. If it looks as if he's blundering, it definitely reflects on him."

Holmes smiled. "Is that *your* view of it?"

"Ultimately, of course, I must think in the same way he does."

"Is that anonymity or self-extinction?" Holmes gave him a glance not unmixed with malice. "With regard to your Munich, I should explain that the point of the exercise should be to associate the Soviets with confining the Chinese to quarters, as it were."

Evelyn gave a little wiggle of excitement.

"This may be precisely the time," Friedlander parried, "when

China can only be persuaded by force—when her revolutionary enthusiasm is such that she will respond to nothing short of coercive military power."

It came out in the voice a pedantic Nazi diplomat might have used on the Czechs or the Austrians. Holmes blinked. "That's called a clarification of position, my dear." Morris was more thin-skinned than he'd thought.

For just a moment Evelyn withdrew her energy from Friedlander and gave it to him.

"What did we do, Morris, when the Soviets asserted their power in Eastern Europe? Or how did the Soviets respond when we overthrew governments in Central America? In Asia, the point is to render conditions sufficiently tolerable for the Chinese that invasion, such as we have just seen, is not necessary. It's a delicate game, but it would be playable, or don't you think so?" Did he have to explain *everything*?

"It may depend on Manse, at least in part, on how hard he pushes."

"Yes," Holmes agreed. Evelyn wiggled again, this time impatiently.

"Morris, I don't want to withhold you from your charming friend. It was lovely meeting you, my dear."

"Stoddard, how good to see you!" It was Ney! His friend indeed stood there in the same blue suit he had worn during the day. "When I heard you were in the game, my first impulse was to call you, but then my conscience said, no, Stoddard will be fearfully busy. But here it is our time."

"Yes, the game is very taxing."

"We all find it so."

"We have done what we could," Holmes said with just a touch of mysticism, or was it fatigue that made his speech sound a bit dreamlike? "You've no doubt heard the President's statement."

"I did," Ney replied. "I thought, a fearful thing it is to head a great country like the United States. I do not know what I would do if this were *my* part. I find mine difficult enough."

Holmes chatted with Ney; the time crept slowly by. "Perhaps," Ney remarked, "when the President says he will use nuclear weapons in forty-eight hours, this is ill-advised. There are those who say the President is too much influenced by Mr. Mikesell and his generals. You, my friend, would know better than I. Would he be so quick to use nuclear weapons in Europe, or is it easier for him to sacrifice people of color?" Ney looked down. "Is this an indelicate question? I feel, perhaps, I have offended?"

"Not at all. My government makes no distinction. Our only aim is the defense of freedom, be it Asiatic or European."

"Yes, you are, it is true, only playing a part in this game," Ambassador Attakor—or was it Ney—said, "but must you go on playing it?"

"Of course, I slip into such a part, if I have one."

"Once a diplomat, always a diplomat, yes?"

"It is late." Holmes said gravely.

"I suppose, I cannot stop myself with my infernal teasing. Even as a schoolboy, I . . ."

"It's late, Ney."

"I'm sorry, I'm disturbing you."

"No, no, it was good to talk." A few minutes later, Holmes noticed that Friedlander was called to the phone, and that he had hastily left. Fatigue suddenly hit him like a wave against a sea wall. Perhaps he had overextended himself. He gave Betty the car keys— she'd stay on—and hailed a cab.

"I'm so tired, I can barely move," Sansone said to his wife as they sat up together in bed. Anne didn't look so hot herself. "Want a nice little round pill?" she asked.

"You know I hate pills. You always pay for them on the other end. What an awful day!"

"I could have invited you to my buyers' conference. It wouldn't have helped, Frank. God, people are dumb, like cows on a doormat."

"Can't find their asses with two hands, huh?"

"You know those shipments I was looking for? Well, they hadn't even been sent. And then as the meeting was breaking up, I twisted my ankle on a piece of carpeting some damn fool forgot to nail down."

He took Anne's ankle in his hand and began to rub it, then started playing back the day as if from a tape recorder. "Anne, ever look around a room and know, just know, that if anything's gonna get done you're the only person who's gonna do it? Well, we were all sitting around today trying to figure out a policy, I mean Manse had promised the President and Defense a plan, but we were all just sitting there doing nothing. Manse, especially, he must have felt down because the President double-crossed him and said we'd use those nuclear weapons right away. I wasn't feeling too good myself, kind of lousy, and I figured, well, what the hell, I'll sit this one out, take it easy. But you know how I am, Anne, I'm like you, I like to get things done. So I made a big pitch for my UN conference, and you know what, it was the only idea they had, so they bought it! Even Holmes backed the idea!"

"That was great, Frank!"

"I was the only one there with any balls."

"My Frank!" Now she giggled.

" 'Course we still got some problems, like who's going to sponsor it, and we still got the President's nuclear threat to worry about." He was getting depressed again. He was probably just tired. "Maybe we'll get that conference and maybe we won't. Shit, we'll probably lose. The hell with it! Let's go to sleep!"

He lay for perhaps five minutes in his usual fetal position. But now he was wide awake, running out into the street lightly clad, looking for pussy. That was it. Christ, Anne would never believe it! He'd come home practically in a box, and now he could feel himself getting an erection! "Anne, are you still awake?"

"Uh-huh. Want me to get you that pill?"

"No, I want *you*."

"You've got to be kidding, Frank. I'm pooped, and my ankle hurts."

"Okay, honey, okay. I just felt like it all of a sudden."

"All of a sudden . . ." Anne said in a drowsy voice, and shifted position.

Cypress trees line a road to a villa. A knight in armor rides with his lance leveled. A diviner's rod, suddenly heavy-tipped, falls to the earth. The old Roman count lies dying with the whore in his villa. She says at the coroner's inquest, "I didn't know, your honor, if he was coming or going." Pains in his chest and stomach. Must be gas. The armored rider falling.

Sharp pain. He could have had one more term if the Blacks hadn't turned on him; one more term and he would have quit. Everything lost. Fear, the leveled lance shining in the sun, the armored man falling. *Ave Maria!*

Riding home in the cab, Holmes reached a moment when he felt as if he were in outer space, timeless, neither here nor there, in moral free-fall. He could admit the outside world, or parts of it, or he could reject it.

He arrived home and let himself in. His dream life loomed as an immense happiness, for his mind could fill the entire world—well, wasn't that the ideal?

He put himself to bed, letting in as little reality as possible. He thanked his wonderfully trained nervous system that asked no questions, that went quietly about its work like maids who never even approach the housekeeper, much less the mistress of the house. His solipsism was complete. In a twinkling he was asleep.

"Is our drafting bee over?" Harrison asked Smith. It was almost three a.m.

"I think that letter looks pretty good," Smith said. "Let's sleep on it, and take a look, say tomorrow morning at eight-thirty. Then I'll try to sell it to the Secretary." He headed for the coatrack. "Thanks, everybody."

He was shaking with fatigue. He turned to the secretary, who had stayed up with them. "Thanks so much." Then to Harrison and Gamarekian, "I'm heading out. Enough of this. Good night."

He picked up his coat and left. The halls were empty, and in the fluorescent light, pale as if from an insult. In the distance, he could hear a machine clunking out speeches and news around the world, monitored by the CIA. What was it this time, Arab propaganda, a famine, a fall of government?

Was any of it real?

What of these telegrams, staff studies, intelligence reports? Just pieces of paper, like any others.

He stepped into an office and sat behind a desk, he didn't know whose. The complete stillness of the building poured into him, and for a moment he was at one with it. Then he was driving his car in mindless, physical motion.

He pulled up to the house. He turned the key and opened the door. Sally Jenks was waiting for him! She'd stayed up the whole night to be there for *him*! He told her everything for half an hour, an hour, he couldn't stop, everything he'd thought about all day, ending with, "But none of it was real!"

"Zach, what do you want to tell me?"

"That . . . that I love you."

"Is that what this all means?"

"Sometimes I just want to run home to you."

She got undressed, and slid in next to him. He'd have wanted to, but he didn't have a thing. She turned toward him, and for just a moment, he put his arms around the real and unreal; then he slept.

☆ ☆ ☆

Outside the State Department, flagpoles stand bare as the necks of condors; in London, like the masts of ships with the dream of great-bellied sails under the sun; in New York, at the East River, like African maidens in a great half-circle, chanting love and war, their rope skirts swaying. In Thailand, they'd be broken in the exhausted wreckage.

Holmes wondered in his sleep if sausages have skins; if a polygon with yet another side would finally become a circle; what a map would be like with a scale of one to one?

Klein looks out his window into the colors of Love—which, he said to himself, has no colors, because Love is a concept.

Smith rides with General Robert E. Lee. At a turn in the battle, grasping the flag, he spurs his horse and gallops into the fray, only to be shot down. As he lies dying, he feels or sees a body emerging from his horse.

Sansone can see from under the lid of a coffin, his brother, Giorgio. The eye that peeps into his from under the lid is the sun!

THE SECOND DAY

Sally Jenks lay in the early morning light that crept under the Venetian blinds. She stirred. She was most beautiful when she made love, and next, when she slept.

"Didn't we just go to bed?" she asked Zach.

"Almost." Her breasts seemed translucent.

"Kiss me before you get up and save the world."

He kissed her on the mouth, and on her beautiful breasts.

"That's better."

"Did you dream?" he asked her.

"Uh-huh. I dreamt we were dancing on a tiled floor, white and black squares, except you could only go up and down, and I could only go on diagonals, so we couldn't dance together."

"You didn't dream that."

"No. Last night, Zach, I dreamt someone was coming at me with a hatchet. It was Peter Jenks, because he did once; that's when I cleared out; I told you. Well, he was at it again."

"Was I there?"

"You're not back where the dreams are, Zach. Here, kiss me again." She lifted her breasts. "They like you, even if they're a bit sleepy right now."

☆ ☆ ☆

BLACK: COMMANDER, US FORCES THAILAND, DECEMBER 8, 1640 HRS, FLASH IMMEDIATE (PASS TO PRESIDENT)

TOP SECRET

DESPITE HEAVY POUNDING BY US AIR FORCE, CHICOM UNITS CONTINUE TO ADVANCE ALONG WIDE FRONT. US AND THAI UNITS UNABLE OFFER SIGNIFICANT RESISTANCE.

☆ ☆ ☆

BLUE: US MISSION UN, DEC 8, 0630 HRS

SECRET

UN SECRETARY GENERAL YULU PHONED TO SAY HE ISSUING CALL FOR IMMEDIATE CEASE FIRE. I POINTED OUT LACK ANY MENTION HIS TEXT WITHDRAWAL CHINESE AND THAT ACCEPTANCE MIGHT APPEAR SADDLE THAILAND WITH PERMANENT CHINESE OCCUPATION. SYG SAID THAT NOT HIS INTENTION, AND THAT ACCEPTANCE CEASE FIRE WLD BE IN HIS VIEW WITHOUT PREJUDICE OTHER ISSUES. HE SAID HE PLANNED GO AHEAD.
SYG SAID HE HOPED RECEIVE OUR REACTION SOONEST. PLEASE INSTRUCT.

KIRKLAND

☆ ☆ ☆

Sansone wasn't sure he was going to get up. He definitely wasn't feeling good, not at all! He didn't need the money *that* much!
Control had woken him up just to read him the goddamn

telegrams. What were they trying to do to him?

The Secretary General was making things worse, but what could you expect? The quality had definitely gone down. First you had that Norwegian—he'd had some balls; but after that, there'd been Hammarskjold, who was a fruit; and then that riceball U Thant; and now—Jesus Christ—they have some character named Yulu!

Not even any mention of a withdrawal! Well, he'd spike that, though maybe (he was putting on his shorts) a cease-fire wasn't all that bad for starters. Hell, right now we were getting our asses whipped! And the cease-fire would make it easier for the Chinese to back down before the nuclear ultimatum, which they hadn't done *yet*.

"Are you statesmen going to accept?" Anne asked.

"Why not," he answered, "if we can talk Defense into it and then the President?" He felt sick to his stomach.

☆ ☆ ☆

WHITE: AMERICAN EMBASSY TEHERAN, DEC 8, 1232 HRS, FLASH IMMEDIATE (PASS TO PRESIDENT)

SECRET

PRIME MINISTER ANSARY CALLED ME IN TO ANNOUNCE REBEL TRIBESMEN HAVE PULLED OFF SEIZURE TABRIZ AND ARE ATTEMPTING EXTEND CONTROL THRU NORTHERN PROVINCES. ARMORED UNITS ARE REPORTEDLY HEADING TO TEHERAN, THO THIS UNCONFIRMED.

REBEL LEADER JAFAR KESHAVARZ HAS ISSUED CALL FOR SOCIALIST REVOLUTION THRUOUT COUNTRY WITH BREAK UP LAND HOLDINGS AND NATIONALIZATION OIL FIELDS.

TRIBESMEN ARE ARMED SOV EQUIPMENT INCLUDING SOME LATE MODEL TANKS. SOV TRAINED CADRES ARE REPORTEDLY IN KEY POSITIONS REBEL

COMMAND, AND LARGE NUMBER SOV ADVISERS ARE RUMORED BE ON SCENE. IMPOSSIBLE ESTIMATE REBEL STRENGTH THIS JUNCTURE.

ANSARY BITTER US DID NOT OFFER SUPPORT AT EARLIER POINT AS URGENTLY REQUESTED. NEVERTHELESS HE BELIEVES STRONG US ACTION EVEN NOW WOULD NEUTRALIZE SOVS AND ENABLE GOV OF IRAN TO OUST REBELS.

NEED INSTRUCTIONS SOONEST.

CUMMINGS

☆ ☆ ☆

AMERICAN EMBASSY MOSCOW, DEC 8, 1203 HRS, FLASH IMMEDIATE (PASS TO PRESIDENT)

TOP SECRET

MOSCOW RADIO MADE BRIEF ANNOUNCEMENT REBEL SEIZURE TABRIZ.

IN ABSENCE INSTRUCTIONS, I HAVE CONFINED MY EFFORTS TO ATTEMPTING SEEK CLARIFICATION. SOVS CONTINUE DISCLAIM ANY KNOWLEDGE THEIR INVOLVEMENT.

MOSCOW STRATEGY WLD APPEAR BE MAINTAIN LOWEST POSSIBLE PROFILE IN IRAN OPERATION WHILE SUPPLYING CADRES AND MAJOR PART EQUIPMENT. WHAT NOT CLEAR THIS JUNCTURE IS EXTENT TO WHICH SOVS WILLING EXERT DIRECT DIPLOMATIC OR MILITARY PRESSURE.

AGAIN I NEED INSTRUCTIONS ON HOW BEST BLUNT ANY SUCH SOV ATTEMPT. EVERY HOUR WE DELAY WE ENCOURAGE SOVS THAT WE UNABLE MEET CRISIS. PLEASE INSTRUCT.

ROLAND

☆ ☆ ☆

Catherine said Michael's thrashing had kept her awake. He'd gotten out of bed, taken up his things, and gone into the other bedroom. Making love hadn't helped him sleep, and now it was almost time to get up.

What difference would it make, he asked himself, if the game were actually taking place? The intellectual content would be the same, and if ultimately that were all . . . But would it make any difference if his plan saved the world, or it saved it only on paper? Didn't the value of a work depend on its quality rather than on its effect? And if that were so, then neither the world nor his plan need be real—well, did they?

He started dressing; he'd have to make his own breakfast. He'd simply imagine the taste of breakfast; why bother to eat it? He felt his face. Overnight, thousands of little hairs had grown up. Little innocents, what did they know of philosophy?

☆ ☆ ☆

Holmes would have preferred not just one *New York Times* but three or four, all starting perhaps at the same point, but rapidly diverging until they gave "all the news that's fit to print" for separate worlds. He might sit through a series of breakfasts, all in white breakfast nooks with severe Scandinavian crockery—timeless, minimalist stuff—until it was well past noon. Time enough then to walk down a street and let reality fall on his train like a shadow. There would be no shadows in the other worlds.

He sat across the table from his wife, whom he had silenced with his lack of attention. He imagined a ghost session of Chinese arguing whether or not they should accept the cease-fire in the face of the American threat. Perhaps when he arrived at the office, there would be word.

As he drove in, Smith remembered his nieces as they had been years ago. They were playing in the back of his mother's house, shrieking in their wet bathing suits in front of the sprinkler. He'd taken Polaroids, dozens of them. Did he remember them, or his pictures of them? Now they had kids of their own. They had grown into cool beauties, had married a lawyer and a college professor, and lived in the suburbs with good tastes and liberal ideals.

How could he feel jealous when they meant so little, even to themselves? Whenever he visited, he must defend the government—his skin like wet putty—against their good liberal shibboleths.

God, all that semen! Something should have come of it, some dark—he didn't have to know—purposeful child, in some foreign country. Just so it was his! How old was Sally Jenks? Forty-one?

When would he be able to call her? How much must be finished! He'd go over the President's letter with Harrison and Alex; and then they'd see the Secretary.

☆ ☆ ☆

At the staff meeting, the Secretary passed around Smith's letter to Rogachev. It was a "commendable piece," he was willing to send it up. Smith was about to suggest the possibility of revision, when the Under Secretary intervened.

"It seems to me," Henderson said, "that we would be sending such a letter at a time when the international atmosphere is completely poisoned. Here we have the Soviets taking over a slice of Iran, and we come to them hat-in-hand asking them to play peacemaker in Thailand?"

"How do you know," the Secretary interjected, "Kuznetsov didn't go to Peking precisely to dissuade the Chinese from intervention?"

"Well, what about their joint communiqué?"

"Well, what about it?"

"It clearly implicates the Soviets in what the Chinese are trying to do. Which, to belabor the obvious, Manse, is to kick us out of the Far East."

"Perhaps. And if so, it would be best, in my view, to seize the opportunity and leave, while we still can with some semblance of grace. As for the Soviets, I shouldn't entirely mind enhancing their reputation as peacemakers in that part of the world."

"The next step then," Sansone said, "would be for us to accept the UN cease-fire. The Chinese have not yet got all that far, and from what we hear, we're not going to be able to drive them back for quite a while. Besides, we've got the five o'clock deadline."

"The tactic to threaten nuclear weapons," Henderson said in a steely voice, "if we let it work, will stop the Chinese cold, and yet it's still too small a provocation to bring in the Soviets."

"Clearly we must accept the cease-fire," the Secretary said.

"You're incredible!" Henderson glared at him.

"I said we will accept the cease-fire!" said the Secretary.

"Yes, yes, accept the cease-fire, accept it, and look like the panty-waisted, effete types people have always said we are. Come on, Manse! Let's stand up for once!"

"I say we accept the cease-fire." Suddenly Vane turned to Sansone. "How do you vote, Senator?"

"Hell, yes!"

"Smith?"

"Yes."

"Holmes?"

"Yes."

"Klein?"

"Sure."

"Well, as Lincoln once said to a recalcitrant cabinet, 'The ayes have it.' There he had a minority of one. Here it is you, Allen, who are isolated. We are accepting the cease-fire."

Henderson backed off—but not before insisting that they make it clear that the cease-fire be conditioned on Chinese withdrawal. If not, the U.S. should be free at any time to start up the war.

The Secretary agreed. They would send up the letter to Chairman Rogachev, and they would accept the cease-fire with Henderson's statement.

The problem, the Secretary concluded, was well in hand. It was 9:25. With an hour before the NSC convened, he left to see the President.

Everyone glanced around at the other members of the staff. Even Henderson had a blinking, incredulous look.

They had a policy: partial disengagement. Whatever you might call it, it was a tangible, definable thing. It had required the imprimatur of the Secretary, but now it had definitely been given.

If it could only be real, thought Klein. They could begin here to undo all the country's mistakes.

Now that they had launched their policy, they waited for word from the Secretary. When it finally came, it was negative. The President had shelved their letter to Chairman Rogachev, at least temporarily, and the Pentagon had blocked acceptance of the cease-fire. The Secretary left word they should join him at the NSC.

Would it always be like that? Holmes, Sansone, even Smith, took the news at that level of expectancy which means to be unflappable, or, in an earlier day, a man of the world. But, Klein thought, if the Secretary were stopped here, when would they ever get to his conference?

The President looked down the long table at the players who constituted the National Security Council, and began. "Good morning, good morning." A few scurried into their seats. "I was thinking, I'm glad I don't have to do this for a living." It fetched only a few laughs. Maybe, Smith thought, the people here were tired. More likely they realized that Mitch Murray wanted the job so bad he could taste it.

"Well," the President bit out, "we don't seem to have gotten anywhere yesterday." He reviewed the situation in Thailand, where the Chinese were now menacing the giant U.S. airbase of Udon Thani; in Iran, where the Soviets had engineered a takeover in the North. "And still we haven't heard a word from the Chinese, or any indication at all if they're prepared to accept the cease-fire. The first question facing us today is, Are we going to accept it ourselves?"

The Secretary of Defense signaled to speak. "A call for a cease-fire was to be expected out of New York. You'll notice, Mr. President, that Secretary General Yulu places no blame on the Chinese or puts any pressure on them whatsoever. So the issue is this: What price are we willing to pay here for a good press? Because if the cease-fire is put into effect now, it will freeze the situation at the point at which our fortunes are lowest. It's simply not in our interests. The decisive military factor is the threat we pose with nuclear weapons."

"That is the reality," Henderson asserted, "and the Chinese have yet to react to it."

Under Secretary of Defense Palmerston joined in. "Once the Chinese realize we mean business, we'll be able to back them out of there."

"Of course, I agree . . ," began the Secretary of State.

"In that case . . ."

". . . that our fortunes in Thailand are indeed at their lowest. But from a moral or even from a military standpoint, they could become much lower. We'll need at least ten days to get reinforcements into Thailand to hold the ground—at least ten days, Mr. Mikesell"—he glanced at him over his Franklin glasses—"to get our troops in Germany and Korea off drugs, while we hurl our nuclear rockets into the towns and villages of Thailand like some impotent cyclops! No, we're not ready to use those weapons. Nor can I place any credence in Mr. Mikesell's argument that because we have nuclear weapons we must, perforce, use them. Indeed, we must avoid using those weapons at all costs. The cease-fire offers precisely such a way. I strongly urge we accept it."

"Will the *Chinese* accept the cease-fire?" the President asked.

"Possibly not, but then . . ."

"If we used nukes from the air," General Curtis cut in, "the situation would be entirely altered, let me assure you." He glanced down at a report. "Weapons fired from the air in the fractional kiloton range would entirely alter the picture. Seek-and-destroy missions could break up any conceivable troop concentrations the Chinese might put together."

"What would they do to the countryside?" asked the Assistant Secretary for Far Eastern Affairs.

"We're fighting a war, Mr. Holmes," said General Curtis.

"Quite!" said Holmes.

"From the political point of view, Mr. President"—it was Vane—"we must avoid using those weapons."

"All right then," said the President, "all right, suppose we go for the cease-fire."

"The difficulty with that," Mikesell returned, "is that the Chinese won't accept it. You'll have given the appearance of having accepted out of weakness."

"I doubt that would be the effect," said the Secretary of State.

"Do you know, do you really know," Smith came in, "what a nuclear weapon can do, even one in the 'fractional kiloton range'? Do you know what a village would look like that got hit with just one of those things?"

"I bet you're going to tell us," Henderson said.

"The whole place would be burning. Parts of bodies strewn around or vaporized, people wandering around in a daze, vomiting. Is that what you want?"

"Okay, okay," the President said, "that's enough, Smith, that's enough. Christ! They'd have the press in there with their goddamn pictures. I'd be seeing 'em for years. You remember Hiroshima? They built a museum with all those pictures of those kids. I mean we may, well, we'll probably have to do it someday, but . . . I don't want to be the one. If people found out, even though it's just . . ." He stopped abruptly and turned to Sansone. "Senator, you can tell the Secretary General we'll accept the cease-fire. What's the next topic?"

The President turned to Iran. Vane was the first to speak. "I understand you've decided to delay the letter Smith drafted to Chairman Rogachev . . . the letter seeking their cooperation in settling the situation in the Far East? Apparently it hasn't cleared your office yet? This would be the time to reconsider it, Mitch."

"Letter? What letter?"

"The letter for your signature to Rogachev, the letter which . . ."

"I killed it," Henderson said.

"You did what?" Vane exploded. "I approved that letter!"

"Considering the Soviets' most recent actions in Iran, I thought withholding the letter was clearly appropriate. Under the circumstances, it might well have proved embarrassing."

"You killed it, and you didn't consult me?"

"Under the circumstances, I felt no need to consult."

"You always consult!"

"The letter," the President said, "it was your idea, right, Smith?"

"Yes, sir."

"Well, I'm afraid, from what you were telling me this morning about it, Allen, it's been overtaken by events." He looked distractedly at Smith. "Good idea, commendable idea." Well, what are we going to do about Iran? You say, Mike, we can send the new Shah some late-model jets, say, eighty or ninety right away to beef up his Air Force?"

"I'm afraid that won't do it," Henderson said. "The Soviets are already there, they're already committed. They could stick in more armaments themselves. If they don't think we're serious about stopping them, we won't be able to."

"Serious?" the President asked. "What do you mean, serious?"

"That we're willing to intervene, to actually go in there ourselves."

"I don't think . . ."

"Henderson's right." It was Smith. What was he saying? "The only way to prevent our having to go in there is to act as if we would. We need to call in their Ambassador and scare the piss out of them!"

Holmes glanced at the Secretary. Vane sat staring at Henderson, but otherwise had no comment.

128

"Okay, Smith, call him in," said the President.

"Yes, sir."

"Well, that's it. I guess our bombs are away," Murray wrapped it up. "'Course, if the Russians or the Chinese take it wrong, we could be in a full-scale war!" Abruptly, he signaled to his aides and left the room.

Henderson approached Smith. "I never thought we'd end up agreeing."

"This is business."

"So our knight has changed camps?"

"Not really."

"This will be amusing. You know, every time you do it, it's like the first time, you have the same feeling, don't you, of risk, of thrill?"

"What are you talking about?"

Henderson put his hands on him again; Smith backed away.

Flying at night, Zach Smith had seen the tracery of dials, the puffs of flak, the lustrous blue-black of the sky. And then the plane shook so that his entire universe had exploded; there was a piece of hot metal in his leg; he was bailing out. Then the glowing thread of his spider silk flew like intestines out of his mouth.

Smith drew arcs on his scratch pad, and dotted lines down to where they intersected. He had lied to Dr. Marvin; he'd paid enough, hadn't he, to earn a little privacy, but then he'd told him . . . about Lorton, about his endless fears.

Martin knew, Sally knew, but how in the hell had Henderson found out?

Dr. Marvin hadn't been there when he had been weak and confused, and had almost done the only thing he'd ever really wanted to do.

Smith was still sitting at the table; almost everyone had left. Klein had been staring at him. Smith rose. Now it was up to him to call in the Soviets.

☆ ☆ ☆

If Smith would only tell him what he'd been thinking. Except, Klein felt, there was immense dignity in holding it back, a dignity which he himself lacked. To talk seemed to him almost obligatory, to put it into words if he knew, or if he wasn't sure, to make that the test. What was Smith thinking about? Why wouldn't he tell him! The unspoken word was like the threat of violence.

Smith seemed disturbed. Men like that climbed towers and killed people. They were all crack shots.

☆ ☆ ☆

Yellow: AP, December 8, Washington, D.C.

NUCLEAR WEAPONS READY IN THAILAND

This morning, additional nuclear weapons were flown in to American units in Northern Thailand. The weapons, the Little John and Honest John rockets and the 8-inch howitzer, have ranges of less than 25 miles, but pack a punch equivalent to hundreds of tons of TNT. The delivery came on the heels of President Murray's declaration at 5 p.m. yesterday that unless the Chinese Communists halted their advance in Thailand within 48 hours, tactical nuclear weapons would be used by the American side.

Defense Secretary Clifford Mikesell explained, "The use of tactical nuclear weapons in Thailand will represent no new departure in American policy. U.S. troops in Europe have been armed with such weapons for years and would have employed them if the Soviets had invaded one of our allies." The Pentagon chief also pointed out that nuclear weapons of the type being deployed in Thailand are no more powerful than strategic bombers which have been in continual use from the early years of the Vietnam War.

☆ ☆ ☆

Yellow: UPI, December 8, Washington, D.C

NUCLEAR PROTESTS SWEEP COUNTRY

A wave of protest swept over the country in reaction to President Murray's threat this morning to use nuclear weapons in Thailand. Quakers, radical pacifists, and even mothers pushing baby strollers joined with college students in marches and demonstrations in over 40 cities.

In Washington, D.C., protesters quickly denounced the President's announcement. Emily Scattergood, Director of the National Ban-the-Bomb Campaign, said a planned rally on the Capitol Mall would draw thousands of citizens. "There is no justification whatsoever in introducing nuclear weapons into the conflict in Thailand," she maintained. "This kind of trigger-happy response is what will plunge us all into nuclear war."

At the University of California at Berkeley, students sat in at half a dozen campus buildings. Over 400 policemen, including members of the National Guard, were necessary to quell the disorders. Similar disturbances marred protests at Antioch and Oberlin Colleges in Ohio, and at the University of Michigan in Ann Arbor.

Would he have been out with the marchers? Klein asked himself. He'd only been to one protest, and then he had bragged to Catherine about it for months. He had not told her how anxious he'd felt. The fact was, the whole business seemed ineffectual; he had better things to do than be miscounted or beaten, and besides, the ban-the-bomb types were intolerably smug.

Except he believed in the causes, in Negro rights—he still couldn't say "Black", in opposing the Vietnam War, in banning the bomb. Nothing could justify nuclear weapons—except yesterday, hadn't he justified them, well, hadn't he, in his flight into *realpolitik* with Holmes?

☆ ☆ ☆

BLUE: US MISSION UN, DEC 8, 1130 HRS

OFFICIAL USE ONLY

AT 1045, US AND THAI DELS ISSUED FORMAL ACCEPTANCE CEASE-FIRE. SECRETARY GENERAL YULU REPORTS CHINESE HAVE GIVEN HIM NO RPT NO INDICATION THEY PREPARED ACCEPT. HE ASKED IF THEY WAITING INSTRUCTIONS. CHINESE REPLIED THEY HAD ALL INSTRUCTIONS NECESSARY BUT WERE NOT PREPARED AT THIS TIME TO ACCEPT OR REJECT CEASE-FIRE.

KIRKLAND

☆ ☆ ☆

Did the Chinese think we were bluffing? Sansone wondered. He felt light, almost weightless, as if nothing mattered now. Maybe they were counting on domestic protest to force the President to back down. Nobody'd listen to it, not in the short term anyway.

His telephone conversations with Kirkland seemed so phoney. Where was Kirkland anyway? The UN Ambassador seemed to be playing it so straight. All of his telegrams, with their resolutions and texts for this and that—in the UN everything seemed to dissolve into resolutions and head counts—what difference did they make?

Did he have a fever? Such a funny world. When Sansone was up in New York, he'd had to blink to believe it. Who the hell would believe there was a country like Gambia or, what was it, Zambia, and black or brown diplomats from God knows where, all dressed up in suits and speaking in French or British accents. It broke him up!

Just as he was getting down to work again, Sansone received a call from Holmes, inviting him to lunch at the Hotel Madison.

Smith and Henderson were ushered into the Secretary of State's office. A few moments later, a Russian was escorted in and introduced. Smith had never seen Ambassador Komplektov before, but if it was all a fake, why did Smith's heart pound as if it would jump out of his body? He could barely hold a cigarette. He wouldn't even try to light it. Smith wiped his forehead with his handkerchief.

"As you are no doubt aware, Mr. Ambassador," Vane began, "regular units of the People's Republic of China have invaded Thailand. Moreover, the Chinese authorities have fully acknowledged the action."

Komplektov waited for the translation, and then spoke in an only slightly accented English. "My government is studying the Chinese action with the same interest, I am sure, as is yours."

Somewhere Smith found a voice in his throat. "We view this action as direct aggression against an ally."

Komplektov smiled. "But there is, I understand, some difference of opinion. The Chinese maintain that Thailand is being used by the United States as a base for aggression against the People's Republic. Such encirclement of a socialist country is not unknown to the Soviet Union."

"Our forces . . ." Smith blocked. "Our forces are entirely defensive in nature."

Vane took it up. "Our forces are stationed in Thailand at the request of the Thai Government, which has, as events have shown, ample reason to fear the Chinese. As you will recall, Chinese forces violating borders is not a phenomenon entirely unknown to your government."

"I am happy to learn your interpretation of the situation."

"We are demanding," Smith went on, "that the Chinese withdraw. They will do that unless they have the assistance of some other major power."

"I can assure you, Mr. Smith, that the Soviet Union is in no way involved, except as a major power concerned in preserving world peace."

Vane lifted his hand to speak. Smith now sat soaked in sweat. Could Komplektov see, could Henderson? "Mr. Ambassador," Vane began, "the President has made clear to the Chinese that if they do not begin to withdraw, we will be forced to use tactical nuclear weapons. I wish to make it clear to *you* that our interests lie entirely in defense. We have no intentions of using these weapons beyond Thailand, or for any other purpose than that of defending Thailand's territorial integrity."

"I will inform Moscow."

Vane continued. "The use of tactical nuclear weapons is, of course, only a last resort. That is why we have given our agreement to the cease-fire proposed by the Secretary General. We wish to avoid using these weapons if at all possible. It is our hope that your government would employ every means to influence the Chinese Communists to accept the cease-fire as well."

"Again, I will inform my government." Again there was no commitment. The meeting was over. There was the Ambassador beginning to gather up his papers. Yet there was Henderson with a smug, expectant look on his face. It was up to Smith. "One more matter, Mr. Ambassador."

"Yes? What else, Mr. Smith?"

"It is clear that the Soviet Union has supplied men and arms to the rebels in Northern Iran."

The Soviet Ambassador shook his head.

Smith glanced at the Secretary, then continued. "We know that native cadres have been trained at a KGB base in Baku, and that they are being sent over the border in considerable numbers. They have brought with them heavy armaments and a considerable number of Soviet military advisers. The United States takes a grave view of these developments."

"*Nyet,* Mr. Smith! *Nyet!* These so-called actions of the Soviet Union you refer to are entirely unknown to me and to my government, as we have already indicated to your Ambassador in Moscow. Why do we need to repeat all this here?"

"Do you deny the takeover in Northern Iran?"

"Mr. Smith, Mr. Smith, the tribesmen in the North have overthrown a tyrannical government with which you are allied. We can sympathize with your unfortunate position. But to blame the Soviet Union for this failure, do not be ridiculous! You are grasping at straws, at mere rumors by those who seek to increase international tensions."

"I'm afraid that in this case the party principally concerned with increasing international tensions is the Soviet Union!"

"I object!"

"Our evidence is hard," Smith said. "The President has personally given us clear directions on this point."

The Soviet Ambassador again shook his head in disbelief.

"Either the Soviet Union fully withdraws its support of the rebellion in Iran and recalls its operatives, or the United States will intervene in force. This could mean, Mr. Ambassador, a full-scale confrontation between American and these Soviet forces. I need not remind you, sir, that the avoidance of such a confrontation has been the object of American diplomacy—as well as Soviet diplomacy—for over twenty years. I needn't remind you of the possible consequences of such a confrontation. Is our position clear, Mr. Ambassador?" Smith stared him right in the face.

"Mr. Smith," Komplektov smiled. "I think you have entirely misjudged the situation. The rebellion in Iran is the spontaneous uprising of oppressed peoples, whose plight the United States has ruthlessly ignored for years."

"Is our position clear?"

Komplektov hesitated. "It is."

"We would appreciate," the Secretary said at last, "your conveying to your government what Mr. Smith has said, as it represents precisely the position of the President of the United States and of the National Security Council."

"I will, Mr. Secretary." Komplektov seemed genuinely shaken.

He finished gathering up his papers, and hurriedly left.

"Nice work," the Secretary said to Smith, but then retreated to his inner office without saying another word.

"It was glorious," Henderson jibed. "Who do you suppose that clown was, anyway?"

"Who knows?"

"Some emigré on the payroll, I bet. Dressed himself up, put a Homburg on his head, and called himself a diplomat."

"He looked pretty real to me."

"Control probably briefed him plenty. Made you nervous, huh? Got a little close in the clinches for you, did it?"

"A little."

"So our knight admits being a little nervous as he enters the lists."

"Fuck off, Henderson!"

After briefing his staff, Smith sat alone in his office. Then, checking that the door was closed, he dialed his wife.

"Honey, this is Zach."

"You sound terrible. You okay?"

"I'm fine, wonderful!"

"Anything wrong?"

"Nothing!"

"I took a nap, and you know what I dreamt?"

"I don't want to hear about your goddamn dreams!"

"Screw up at work?"

"You shut up! You just shut up! It went right, it went perfectly. You want to think I fucked up, you want to think that, but I didn't. I didn't. I did it right!" He found himself starting to cry on the phone. He hardened his voice. "I did fine. I was supposed to scare the piss out of 'em, and I did. I just can't do it anymore. I can't do this kind of thing unless it's real, not some goddamn dream! I feel like somebody's painted my face, like I'm wearing lipstick and rouge and eye makeup."

"If it wasn't for me, you'd be wearing that stuff now!"

"I never, I never put on makeup!"

"I'm sorry. I didn't mean to say that, I'm sorry."

He said nothing.

" Zach?"

"Fuck off!"

"You like *me* to wear makeup, don't you?"

"You're a woman. That's what women do."

"You mean, we fake it. That's what makeup is, faking it, right?"

"Yeah, you fake it. You did plenty of that, didn't you, when you worked the Hill?"

"You've done a lot of faking yourself!"

"No, not that. I never . . ."

"We've both done things we don't like—only I don't blame you now. You dropped bombs on people, Zach, people who'd never done a damn thing to you. You didn't even know who they were. I've never done that, but I don't go around forgiving *you* all the time."

"No, look, it's done, it's done. I'm sorry, honey."

She was still shouting and crying, "I can't do anything about what happened before! You married me, cause you loved me!"

"It doesn't matter, it doesn't."

"You know, Zach"—her mood had changed, or was she still faking it?—"I might have liked knowing you in my first life. We'd have married in some foreign place, like an embassy? Where, where would it be?"

"My first post was Budapest."

"Okay, Budapest. But then maybe you wouldn't have married me. I wouldn't have known which fork to hold my hand with."

"'Which fork to hold your hand with?'"

"You would have wanted me, Zach. When I was young, I was something else."

"You still . . ."

" No, I'm okay, you tell me that."

". . . I try not to think about my life," Zach said, "the way I was before I met you, though I do sometimes."

"You and Dr. Marvin."

"Yes, Dr. Marvin."

"I don't like him."

"You've told me."

"He's like a girl you've laid, and I'm glad it was good for you, but it isn't me. It's like he's sitting there all the time telling you I wasn't there, that I wasn't part of your life then, the part that mattered."

"No, no, that's wrong," Zach said. "I love you *now*."

"Zach, I . . ."

"Would you like to have a kid?"

"What?"

"Do you want to have a baby?" Where had that come from? Why had he said that?

"You're serious!"

The rage was coming back; he'd have to be careful. "I just said it!"

"I didn't know."

"I just said it!"

"I heard you."

"Do you want one?"

"All right, Zach." She sounded bitter, angry. "I'll see you tonight. I got to go." She hung up.

Smith walked down to the river and strolled along the stone embankment looking across to Virginia. He wondered how far it went up. The Potomac was so wide when it reached Washington. Theodore Roosevelt Island was somewhere near, and farther up was Great Falls. The Potomac was chemical, green, and bubbling like a lye bath. Another river he'd paddled in his canoe three hundred years ago, when the Indians were here.

He laughed to himself. He'd have shot them all!

He'd have a kid.

He'd take him for a ride in his bomber, and let him push the button.

If it were only night. A cleaver slashed into the melon green hills across the river!

☆ ☆ ☆

BLUE: US MISSION UN, DEC 8, 1134 HRS

SECRET

SAW FEDEROV 1100 AND ASKED HIM STRAIGHT OUT IF SOVS COULD SUPPORT BELGIAN TEXT. FEDEROV SAID USSR COULD DEFINITELY NOT RPT NOT SUPPORT CONDEMNATORY RESOLUTION. LIMIT THEY COULD GO WAS TO QTE REGRET UNQTE PRESENT SITUATION AND TO QTE CALL UPON ALL PARTIES TO OBSERVE AN IMMEDIATE CEASE FIRE PENDING A MORE PERMANENT SETTLEMENT OF THE PROBLEMS. UNQTE.

I SAID THIS CONDONED CHINESE AGGRESSION AND FROZE ITS OCCUPATION THAI TERRITORY. FEDEROV SAID HE WAS SYMPATHETIC IMMEDIATE US POSITION BUT FELT IT HIGH TIME ABSURDITY US OVERCOMMITMENT IN FAR EAST BE BROUGHT HOME. WLD CHINA HAVE INVADED IF US WERE NOT USING THAILAND AS MAJOR MILITARY BASE? WHAT HAD BEEN US RESPONSE IN GUATEMALA, CUBA, ETC?

MOVING DOWN I ASKED IF SOVS COULD BACK OPERATIVE PARA CALLING UPON ALL PARTIES TO ATTEND CONFERENCE ON AREA SECURITY. FEDEROV SAID HE AWAITING INSTRUCTIONS.

KIRKLAND

☆ ☆ ☆

To lunch, Holmes told himself after reading the latest cables. He crossed Virginia Avenue to find Sansone waiting for him in the lobby of the Madison.

"Glad to see you, Senator. How are you faring in this hectic business?"

"Not bad, not bad, though it's quite a pressure cooker. I'm frankly impressed by the whole arrangement."

"Yes, it *is* striking."

"What do you think it all costs?"

"In the millions, I'd say."

"You think that much?"

"I don't imagine your services come for nothing"—Holmes gave a sly wink—"and they haven't spared expenses in other areas as well. It's quite elaborate."

"I'll be frank, my last run for the Senate left me with quite a few debts. Trouble with politics these days is that it costs a mint to get elected, and once you're in, you're constantly struggling to make it up."

"I imagine, Senator, that's one advantage of being a civil servant, although I doubt *I* could have been elected to anything."

"Not at all, not at all! I never thought I'd be in politics myself until the state machine decided they wanted a reform candidate. Frankly, they were starting to stink a little, so they ran me for State Senator. After that, I never looked back." He smiled, then shook his head. "Well, maybe you're right, maybe certain people *do* have a knack for it.

They went through the martinis and into lunch. The Senator told Holmes the story of his political career, his first speeches, about the boss, D'Antonio. "I used to wonder what he would ask from me, but he never asked much, well not *too* much, although it always made me nervous." Holmes could imagine. Light was slanting in from a window, putting in sharp relief the glasses and plates on the table, making it almost impossible for Holmes to see Sansone's face. "Well, now I'm trying something new," the Senator concluded. "Though you probably knew I was up at the UN one year as a public member, so it's not *that* new."

"I imagine it comes back easily enough," Holmes said. "I feel like an old horse slipping into harness myself."

"It's hard work. 'Course, when I was in office, we had days just as bad as this, even worse. I guess today, though, I'm just not feeling up to it. Must be coming down with something. It's that . . . There's something crazy about it. You start believing in it. Like this whole business in the Far East right now, or in Iran. It all seems plausible to me." He shook his head. "Must be hard just to quit."

"Are you thinking of dropping out?"

"No, no, not at all. I'll be around for awhile."

Sansone signaled for the waiter, and paid the bill over Holmes's mild protests. "Well," the Senator said, "I suppose we'd better get back. I've got a resolution coming up, the one condemning the Chinese. We're going to give it a whirl."

They headed out the Madison. Before Sansone, Holmes felt like the slenderest of *toreros*, perhaps a toy one made of pipe cleaners.

Smith turned back to walk along the Reflecting Pond until he reached the Washington Monument. The temporary buildings had long since gone. The tempos, as they were called, had grown up in the war, like shanty towns in South Africa. Would they crop up again in the next war?

The mound leading up to the Monument, despite the season, was green and mossy. He lay down in his top coat looking up. "Five hundred fifty-five feet tall, which sways ten inches in a thirty-mile wind," the guide had said about that obscenity with its red eye. From the top, Washington looked misty, topographic, unreal.

He got to his feet, skirted the White House, then walked up 16th Street.

On his right was the Soviet Embassy. He'd last been there to see a film about a man bringing a bear to Moscow from the Caucasus, a stupid farce, at the end of which he'd clapped politely with all the other diplomatic guests. He went in. A woman with tight blond hair behind the reception desk asked him what he wanted. Her voice was that of an Aeroflot stewardess cruising at twenty thousand feet.

"Ah'm just a tourist, ma'am, from Texas," Smith said, "and ah jest wanted to see what the inside of the Soviet"—he drew out each syllable—"Embassy looked like, so ah could write home and tell the folks." The receptionist smiled, looked at him quizzically. Was she about to call a guard? He glanced quickly around and left.

At the last minute, Michael Klein asked Carolyn Carr out to lunch at the Madison. "Of course, Professor." Carolyn was dressed professionally, if somewhat provocatively, in a short-skirted suit with a fluffy, almost Elizabethan blouse. An attractive woman; was she a divorcée? She smiled in a way which reminded him of a graduate student he'd slept with years ago. It was during a summer session at SUNY Binghamton—Sheila, Susan, he couldn't remember her name.

They ordered drinks. Klein told her about the series of academic appointments which had made up his life, imputing connection and purpose when there'd been so little. "It's always seemed the height of romanticism to know exactly what you want to do," he said. "I've always been surprised, relieved, actually, to learn just how purposeless the lives of most other people have been."

"*You* sound like you've always known what you wanted."

"I suppose," Klein said. "And you, when you were a little girl and people were talking to you about being a nurse, or a housewife, were you imagining yourself pleading a case before the Supreme Court?"

"Oh, Michael"—she was already becoming more familiar. "After my divorce, I did a little canvas of the professions, and it struck me that in just three years of law school, I could put myself in a position to make a pile of money." She told him, though, that at Phelps & Wyatt, she had a cubicle like all the other young lawyers; she never saw clients, didn't know what one looked like. She made enough to live pretty well, she had no complaints about that. In answer to his questions, she said she rarely went out, hated Washington though she'd lived here nine years. Her ex was with the Securities and

Exchange Commission. "Just thinking about him makes me shudder." She giggled. "Michael, you won't write me up as a lush if I have another drink, will you? It was so nice of you to invite me to lunch. I was imagining you'd be some stuffy fogy with academic keys. What a relief you've turned out to be!"

"Oh you, too. You, too." Was he blushing?

They started talking about his plan for a conference. "I loved your article," she said. "You wouldn't happen to have a copy of your book I could look at? Go to the source, is what my law professors used to say."

Klein made a you-must-be-kidding face; she took his hand. "No, I'd really like to see it. I'll just curl up with it in bed."

Klein asked, "Do you get the feeling that what you're doing right now, I mean, in the game, is real?"

"Not yet, but that's always true in a new job. It takes a little while until that begins to happen."

"Even if it doesn't," Klein said, "I find the people interesting." Her office-mate, Jay Wyzanski, he told her, was a tough guy who'd make a great police-court lawyer. Carolyn said he wasn't tough at all, but cuddlesome, like a bear. How did she like Holmes, that "lean-shanked relic of the eighteenth century?" Klein imitated Holmes's Johnsonian manner. She gave a delicious laugh.

"Can I interest you in a drink after work?" she asked him. "Do you like Pimm's; they're an enthusiasm I picked up in London."

"Pimm's. Of course." He had no idea what it was.

"I have an exotic assortment of fruits and vegetables I put in. I'm famous for them." She had an efficiency at the Coronado, just three blocks away.

When Smith returned to his office, there was a copy of a letter from Chairman Rogachev in his in-box. He felt a weak flicker of interest for whatever might be its Byzantine import. But he didn't open it, not yet. His astral body was outside setting fires, while in several hallways on silver trays lay embossed announcements of births and deaths. He lit a cigarette, then picked up the letter.

☆ ☆ ☆

Purple: Letter of R.V. Rogachev, Chairman of the Council of Ministers of the USSR, to Mitchell Murray, President of the United States

TOP SECRET

Dear Mr. President:

It is often useful for the leaders of great countries to communicate with one another directly and openly. I recall with the greatest pleasure our meeting last May in Vienna, although, in frankness, less resulted from that meeting than perhaps we wished. Yet there was a gain in understanding, was there not? I have read your letter of December 8 as an effort to build upon that foundation.

The events in Thailand are as disturbing to the Soviet Union, Mr. President, as you indicate they are to the United States, although, without doubt, we may view them in a different manner.

I believe the first step to a return to peace in Thailand, and perhaps in all of Southeast Asia, will be a cease-fire as the Secretary General of the United Nations has suggested. I have today written to Chairman Shih-Ying Chen to urge acceptance by the People's Republic of China. However, I have no assurance that such a cease-fire is acceptable to China at this time.

Once this cease-fire is secured, the Soviet Union will sponsor a conference in Moscow to discuss general questions of security and economic cooperation in Southeast Asia. This conference will attempt to substitute for the present unacceptable security arrangements others which will allow all the peoples of Southeast Asia to live in peace and amity, with the sure guarantee of the larger powers having geographical proximity in the area.

Allow me, Mr. President, to express my kindest personal respects.

Sincerely yours,

R.V. Rogachev
Chairman of the Council of
Ministers of the U.S.S.R.

☆ ☆ ☆

So, Zach thought, Rogachev, or whoever he was, had gone ahead with a letter of his own inviting *us* to a conference *in Moscow,* with the United States shoved out of any security arrangements. Nor was there a word about the Chinese withdrawing from Thailand, or anything, anything at all, about Iran—as if Zach's confrontation with the Soviet Ambassador had never even taken place.

"He's one smart mother," was Harrison's comment. He'd caught Rogachev's take-charge manner.

"Should the President go back to him?"

"He's got to now."

☆ ☆ ☆

Delightful! Rogachev's letter was just what Holmes had expected. He positively skipped into his aides' office, but Randolph and Mary were out canvassing the Asian allies. It was a bit of a relief for Holmes's still-lingering Puritan conscience to know that while he'd fiddled, Rome had not really burned. Or did it matter? At Panmunjom, at the end of the Korean War, he'd been on the negotiating team sitting at the peace table, with its white line running down the middle. All those months; they'd seemed interminable, while the Chinese and Koreans dispatched insults daily at the U.S. delegation. They were "toadies," "lackeys," "militarists." They had "lied," "despoiled," and so on—all in endless, repetitive set pieces, as the fighting went on and thousands died, and prisoners rotted, were brainwashed, or beaten. The American delegation had almost collapsed, apparently from the pressure and humiliation. For Holmes, when he was not occasionally amused by the stupidity of his adversaries, the proceedings were simply a boring game. He had taken the solicitude with which he was treated upon his return with mild incredulity.

What did the Soviets want; how much could they wring out of our side? They didn't hold that many cards. The draft letter from the President, now that Holmes thought of it, had overstated our need of them. Rogachev, by the same token, had assumed far too much. It would take several exchanges to set matters aright. And then? He found his mind curiously blank.

After his lunch with Carolyn, Klein resumed his official tone with her—*bien entendue.*

He began reading the material in his in-box. There was the letter from Chairman Rogachev.

What would Carolyn look like in bed? He'd wowed her, or maybe she was just a woman who slept with anyone who interested her. Why not; if you were good-looking like Carolyn, you could do whatever you wanted, and ask questions later. It was 2:25.

So the Russians were trying to take over his conference. Wouldn't that kill it?

Even the drinks didn't help. Sansone was getting pains again in his chest and stomach. When he'd lost the nomination—after all those years, his own party, his own fucking party, had dumped him!—Dr. Schultz had been glad. "Will do you good to relax, a man in your condition; it's time you quit, Senator." He'd told Sansone not to eat so much, stop smoking, drinking—it was all a strain on his heart.

But wasn't life a strain on one's heart? Not for people like Holmes. They didn't seem to care.

Holmes was married to that endless phonograph record. What was her name? Betty. Did they have kids. Did they ever make love? Jesus!

He'd have to get down to work.

Sansone hung up his coat, then looked in his in-box. There it was, the letter from Rogachev sitting in the box probably the whole time he was having lunch.

Who'd written it? What would it say? Would it change what they were doing at the UN? His afternoon was cut out for him, that was for sure!

Smith got Morris Friedlander on the line. The President, Friedlander said with a smug proprietorial tone, felt that Rogachev was trying to take him for a ride. "Our President is going to let Chairman Rogachev know exactly where we stand."

"Where's that, Morris?"

"Before he'll agree to a conference, any conference, he wants 'every Chinaman' —I'm quoting him, Zachariah—'every Chinaman,' isn't that delightful?—out of Thailand. And there isn't 'going to be any arrangement that doesn't include the U.S. of A.,' got that? Indeed, he will shortly be sending the Chairman our firm reply. He's asked me to draft it. I shall give it the full force of his convictions."

Smith rang up the Secretary to warn him that the President might blow any negotiations with Rogachev, on Thailand *or* Iran, if the Secretary didn't tone him down.

Over the phone, Smith detected the Secretary's sigh. "I suppose I must call him right away. Thank you, Zach."

Frank Sansone had drafted the telegram to New York. Wylie had cleared it through; presumably it was out. It instructed Kirkland to force a vote on a UN resolution condemning the Chinese, which the Soviets would then veto. And still the Chinese had said nothing about the cease-fire.

Well, all *his* pins were lined up.

☆ ☆ ☆

WHITE: WORLD MONITORING SERVICE, DEC 8, 2105 HRS
FLASH IMMEDIATE (PASS TO PRESIDENT)

OFFICIAL USE ONLY

OPEN TELEGRAM TO MITCHELL MURRAY, PRESIDENT OF THE UNITED STATES, FROM SHIH-YING CHEN, ACTING CHAIRMAN OF THE CENTRAL COMMITTEE OF THE PEOPLE'S REPUBLIC OF CHINA

SIR: THE PEOPLES OF SOUTHEAST ASIA HAVE ENLISTED UNDER THE BANNER OF COMMUNISM TO FREE THEMSELVES FROM WESTERN COLONIALIST OPPRESSION. THERE IS NOTHING THE UNITED STATES AND ITS ALLIES CAN DO TO STOP THE MARCH OF THE AWAKENED PEOPLES.

ANY ATTEMPT BY THE IMPERIALISTS TO USE NUCLEAR WEAPONS TO PREVENT THE LIBERATION OF THAILAND WILL BE MET WITH INSTANT RETALIATION BY THE NUCLEAR FORCES OF THE PEOPLE'S REPUBLIC OF CHINA.

YOU, SIR, MUST DECIDE WHETHER TO GIVE UP YOUR INSANE COLONIALIST SCHEMES OR FACE THE SURE DESTRUCTION OF YOUR ARMIES AND CITIES.

BLACK: COMMANDER, US FORCES THAILAND, DEC 9, 0210 HRS FLASH IMMEDIATE (PASS TO PRESIDENT)

TOP SECRET

UDON THANI AIR BASE FELL 0100 HRS BEFORE MASSIVE ASSAULTS 12TH AND 23RD CHINESE ROUTE ARMIES.

WITH MAJOR BASES OF RESISTANCE ELIMINATED, SITUATION NORTHERN AND CENTRAL THAILAND EXTREMELY SERIOUS. UNLESS WE ABLE DEFEND OUR UNITS WITH NUCLEAR WEAPONS MASS DESTRUCTION WE SEE NO HOPE . . .

Defense and the Joint Chiefs kept to themselves, talked in low voices. Smith tried to open up General Curtis, but got a "Let's wait and see how it shakes down, Smith." Of the State Department team, only Henderson seemed *persona grata* with Defense. Where Klein grew up, the boys who were the big fighters were also the big braggers. That was part of it, to humiliate your opponent. Usually you didn't *have* to fight—but the Defense types must have grown up in a different neighborhood.

It was starting up all over again, Smith thought, the Secretary in the chair, the rigid figures sitting along the sides of the table. "I trust," the Secretary began, "you will soon see the President's firm reply to Chairman Rogachev." Was there a hint of irony in the Secretary's voice? "Mr. Mikesell, you and General Curtis seem to have laid claims to areas which extend well beyond the military, but for the moment may I confine you to that sphere? I trust you can enlighten us concerning that situation, at least."

"Maybe," the Secretary of Defense replied, "you haven't read the recent cables. We've just lost Udon Thani. We've lost over 5,000 men. Our planes barely got off the ground. If we'd used nuclear weapons, Udon would not be in Communist hands today, and we would still be in command in Northern Thailand.

"The Free World has already lost enormous prestige by its weakness in Thailand. But we can still recover our position if we use the sophisticated weapons we now have to stop the Communists before they achieve a momentum of victory. Under present circumstances, a conventional war with the Chinese is a luxury we cannot afford.

"You've all heard what the Chinese have to say." Mikesell's eyes scanned the faces of the men seated around the table. "The Chinese don't intend to back down. If we use nuclear weapons, they can retaliate with nuclear weapons against our armies and cities. I propose, and I have the complete concurrence of the Joint Chiefs, that we go in immediately with a surprise missile attack, strictly conventional, on their missile facilities. These attacks can be followed up by bombing raids. Simultaneous raids on Chinese airfields will also neutralize any possibility . . ."

What was he saying? Smith could hardly hear it, though he caught the main drift.

General Curtis had taken it up. "A surgical attack of this kind could immediately neutralize their entire missile force. We have a technical study here of the feasibility of such a preemptive raid." What were they talking about? Did they know what they were doing? "The risk is minimal, and the gains . . ."

They were going to blow everyone up! "What if our intelligence is faulty," Smith asked, "or some of their missiles get loose? Our ABM system won't work—you know that! It's never worked! At least now there's a *chance* the Chinese will back down!"

"A surgical strike, such as we are suggesting," General Curtis continued, ignoring Smith completely, "is the safest policy we have at this point in time."

"They won't take it! They could end up destroying half our cities! And what about the Soviets? Are they just going to *sit* for this? Have you even *thought* about that?" Smith was shouting.

"We're talking about a strictly surgical strike, Mr. Smith." Even as he was shouting, Smith knew it wasn't real, that the whole business was going on in another dimension.

"What you are doing by this action," Klein broke in, "is changing the rules of the game."

"We aren't the ones who changed the rules," Mikesell answered.

Holmes smiled. "Mr. Mikesell, when this game is over, under your conception of the rules, will there be any players left?"

An hour later, the meeting ended; there was no compromise. They would have to go to the President.

The reports from Thailand were getting worse. Thick red arrows pierced into the green of the map. How many miles? A hundred, a hundred twenty-five? Despite American pressure, the Thais were still fighting very little. American units were falling back, but several more had been overrun, destroyed, or captured. In less than twenty-four hours, Smith thought, they'd get authority to use nuclear weapons. That would be five a.m., Bangkok time, almost dawn!

He wouldn't be there.

He'd be in some non-world, somewhere else, if only behind a door, in a cellar, deep in the ground, while the atomic dawn broke over his head, and over the whole landscape!

When Smith got back to the office, Harrison and Gamarekian had just put together the results of the NATO Council meeting which had ended in Brussels an hour ago. The NATO ministers had lined up behind the U.S. Six countries had even expressed a willingness to kick in troops.

"Not bad," Harrison said, "even *with* the arm twisting."

"Suppose not," Smith said.

☆ ☆ ☆

As he walked back, Klein remembered the meeting in the Secretary's office that morning when the State Department team had agreed on a policy. It seemed now so far away, or rather, out of sight, like one of those valley villages in the Alps that one discovers, with its little church and nestled houses and clink of bells, but never finds again.

They hadn't changed. State's position was still the same. But Udon Thani was a defeat. Was that the problem? If their policy had been adopted, Udon would have been lost anyway. Yet it was a defeat, because the rules had not yet been changed, the policy was not yet "partial disengagement." Nobody yet measured wins and losses that way.

What time was it? Six o'clock. How should he arrange to go to the Coronado? He dialed Catherine.

"Darling, this is Michael."

"You sound strange. Is that really you?" she asked.

"Who do you think it is?"

"Well, your voice is all dried out. I think you imagine you're really *in* the State Department, and you're trying to sound diplomatic. Am I right?"

"No, I was just calling to say that I'll be home late. We're still at it in the Security Council, and some other things have come up." What could he say? "I really have to go. Don't wait up."

☆ ☆ ☆

Sansone sat in his office listening to Kirkland's voice over the intercom as he presented the U.S. case in the UN. There wouldn't be a vote on the Belgian resolution until at least seven-thirty, and then it'd be another hour or two before they got to the cease-fire. Nine o'clock, maybe ten. It wasn't fair to stick Tucker and Wylie again.

He saw a row of suspended metal balls. Suspending the ball at the far end, he let it crash into the row. Nothing came out at the other

152

end. There was a crash and everything had gone dead!

Sansone lurched to his feet. "I'm going to dinner. Wylie, why don't you and Tucker go home. *I'll* stay here tonight."

☆ ☆ ☆

The telephone rang. "Ambassador Holmes, please hold for the Secretary."

Then, "Holmes, I'm calling to tell you the result of my talk with Mitchell Murray, or should I say the President. He is taking it all rather seriously, but then, I suppose, perhaps it's best he does. In any case, he's decided to make a strike against the Chinese missile facilities and airfields, but he's persuaded to wait until the five o'clock deadline."

"Have you told the others?"

"My secretary's doing so, if they're available. Smith called *me.*"

"I suspect," Holmes said, "it would be easier for the Chinese to accept the cease-fire if they had a good excuse. For example, we might offer them . . ."

"It's late, Holmes."

"Yes, it is."

"And besides, my dear fellow, one can't count on someone as resourceful as yourself being in this game, which is why your retirement should be considered such a loss to the Service. It might just be better at this point that we do nothing."

"How so?" asked Holmes.

"It will be more interesting that way," said the Secretary.

"Of course." Holmes smiled. "I'm so glad you called. Good-night."

☆ ☆ ☆

"I'll come up a little later," Klein told Carolyn Carr.

"Don't be silly." Together they walked out of the State Department Building and over to the Coronado, which rose high above the reconstructed town houses of Foggy Bottom. In the lobby, a plant with huge supplicating leaves twisted its tree-thick stem out of a pot.

The elevator was carpeted, wood-paneled, and silent. Carolyn turned the key in her apartment door. "And now, Professor Klein, I'll fix you the most fantastic Pimm's." And she disappeared.

What was happening in the game right now? Klein wondered. Was the Chinese team deciding to accept the cease-fire? Would there be a nuclear war? Carolyn came back with the drinks. She was wearing lounging pajamas, low cut in the front, with swishing pants.

"Nice place."

"You really like it?"

"Yes, very much." He noticed it for the first time. The decor was *fin de siecle* camp.

The drinks were good—cucumbers, oranges, apples, with the heavy, brown taste of a liqueur he'd never had. He was on his second. "Tell me what it was like." She described taking acid when she was an undergraduate at Wesleyan. She hadn't been afraid, despite all its risks, of entering another reality. He put his arm around her, and in a moment they embraced.

She carefully set down her drink, and laughed, "Okay, Professor," and disappeared again, to come out this time in a transparent nightie. Everything went easily, although in the back of his mind, it seemed in slow motion or too fast.

The nightie was a nice touch.

Afterwards, as they talked, her voice grew sleepier. Was she just reacting protectively to his sounding bored? She explained that when she'd been married, her husband had been getting his MBA. Maybe it was living in graduate student housing. They'd been in the swing and everyone had known about their problems until they just didn't have their own lives anymore. A year or so later they'd separated, and finally divorced.

Klein tried to slow down, as, when a little boy, he'd tried to walk at the speed of his grandmother. He waited until the end of Carolyn's story. "I'm sorry, but I really have to go." She gave him a look, not to see, he thought, if sex had made any difference for him, she was too modern for that, but if he, someone, *cared* about her? "It was marvelous," he said. "I'm sorry I've got to go."

"It's okay."

He'd come back in, closed the door, and kissed her hard. Then he was on the street, heading back to the State Department.

Fortunately, Holmes had found the foresight to make reservations, even if he'd forgotten to inform his wife. He waited while Betty dressed in one of those Connecticut Avenue creations that hovered between Hattie Carnegie and Roman matron. He had wanted the ritual of a Chinese meal, the even-tempered passage from course to course, the ladling, sipping, tasting, but most important, the sitting, when the mind did not so much resist thought as simply delight in the energetic void of its possibilities. Connected thought was tiresome, and even chit-chat or gossip could hardly claim pretense to the sublimity he sought now.

Betty always twitched. Holmes had disciplined himself to ignore this, but when the meal was over, he inexplicably wanted to do something nice for her. Maybe tonight, for their social calendar was a blank, he would take her to a movie. He would see anything. "Your choice, my dear," and he meant it. "Anything."

If they were going to bomb China, Smith thought as he drove home, there would be a full-scale war.

He remembered a recurring dream. He was driving a car up a road which became steeper and steeper, until suddenly he realized he was on the rising half of a drawbridge. Would he make it to the other side? Now the bridge became almost vertical. He'd tumble back and plunge into the water! The dream was wrong! Like a child who wakes up crying from a nightmare, and gradually realizes that his dream is not there, or not true, Zach felt somehow cheated.

Sally Jenks was waiting for him. "Did you really mean it about having a kid?" Her voice sounded at the same time giddy and determined.

"I said I did."

"Then let's do it!"

"Right now?"

"I didn't put in my diaphragm." She actually started unbuttoning her blouse.

Why couldn't she have waited for drinks and dinner, and seduced him? Or would that have been worse? Because as he pulled out his tie, he knew it wouldn't be any good. He saw Sally in harsh light. He saw her lying there waiting for a tube to go up her cunt!

"Here, lover. Kiss me." Her hands moved down his pants and brushed his cock. He felt numb.

"Honey, let's have a drink first. I just got back from the office. I want to . . ."

"Sure, what'll it be? A Jack Daniels? I'll get undressed though. I love you, Zach. I know you love me. I want a kid. I thought about it all day, and I want one. And you want one, too, you big stupe!"

"Okay then, okay, let's make love."

"No, let's have a drink." She finished undressing, and paraded back and forth completely nude with the ice-tray, water, and the Jack Daniels. She sat by him on the bed, and they drank.

"Feel better?"

"Uh-huh." Did he? She came up behind him and undid his buttons; he could feel her pressure but he didn't look back. He turned out the lights, and addressed himself to her body, which lay like a continent up from a sea of sheets.

Her cunt was waiting. He caressed her; said he wouldn't think about himself; wanted the kid; loved her, "Sally Jenks;" felt something and tried to go in, but there was nothing.

She lay with him quietly, her hand holding his cock, which buzzed like flies. Sometimes when Sally stood with her back to the sunlight she glowed so that her blond hair fused into the light. He felt hard, and at the same time a stab of panic, and plunged in. He came almost instantly.

Sally suddenly seized him. They clung together. Sally began to cry.

He would have to begin all over again, to make love as an adolescent, shy and unsure. But he'd do it, he and Sally Jenks. And the child, it would be possible now, or probable, or maybe even real!

They'd go out to dinner, it didn't matter where, so they spent a lot of time arguing about it, and then they laughed, and said "Eanie, meanie, minie, moe," and went Hungarian.

There was the black night against Sally Jenks's white leather coat. Smith held her hand. She'd changed in just that evening. She was more substantial, was that it? Less cut out, less like a cartoon of *The Great American Nude*. His own voice was louder, he was almost afraid to touch her!

Later they went dancing at a soul place on 12th Street. Sally Jenks said she'd known the owner before whites could go to places like that. Had she had some kind of business arrangement there? When she introduced him, the owner said, "Okay, Mr. Smith," and gave a little stomp or shrug, not unfriendly, just noncommittal. She might have married a Black man, Smith thought, but she married *me*. The place was bare and dirty, with liquor signs on the walls. No one was there now except a couple of young musicians in headbands and T-shirts, who made their music like cats facing each other in some hidden rhythm of intimidation.

Sally Jenks and he began to dance. She barely moved, just tilted and eased, shook every once in a while. What kind of juice did she squeeze? He kept in, and tried not to be hurt by all that beauty. That she loved him, that hung on the outside, as she danced with that total lyrical absorption of youth giving up its life in a war.

She shook now plenty, and laughed, and was genuinely obscene. Suddenly she shouted angrily, "Let's go!" But they had done it. They drove home. Their car was like a gondola!

Holmes emerged with his wife from the film, which stayed in the back of his mind as a long, luminous stretch of beach.

She'd enjoyed it, she said.

He was glad. The car glided along the luminous strand. When he was home, he unbuttoned, brushed, washed, pissed, flushed, and finally kissed, as if this were taking place in the apartment below. Behind the moon, a dragon stretched and revealed an astonishing length of tail. Not mine, Holmes thought, and while Betty was still sitting up in bed, he slept.

☆ ☆ ☆

Senator Sansone sat in his office listening to the vote on the resolution condemning the Chinese Communists: 7 to 3 to 1. They'd just made it, although, of course, the Soviet veto meant that officially they hadn't.

Well, he thought, even if we were getting a licking in Thailand, his end was going okay. They were making their points in the UN, regardless of whatever *else* was happening. He'd done *his* part.

He could always produce. Give Frank Sansone a job and he'd get it done. It was something young people didn't do anymore. Give them a job and they'd ask, What for? Because otherwise the milk didn't get delivered, the trains didn't run, not just on time, they didn't run at *all*, that's why!

If they knew what they were talking about, if they'd done their homework, he'd have more respect for them. They were supposed to be political. But all this business of dressing up and freaking people out, as they called it. Politics was a serious business. He'd spent his entire life in it. Even if those kids were on his side, he wouldn't have had 'em. He saw them in their costumes surrounding him like some horror crowd, a witches' Sabbath.

He laughed. There he was late at night playing a no-count game with gas in his chest. He sat back in his swivel chair. He loved himself!

What if he'd cared for Carolyn Carr, Klein thought; it'd be worse, wouldn't it? He lay in a hot tub reading a study of the Red Shield. He and Catherine would fight, not because she knew, but because he was irritated that he was guilty or wrong. Why should she suffer? If she never found out, it wouldn't have happened. Only the price he must pay this time would be not to tell her.

He'd stopped the car at the Negro's flower stand on Dupont Circle. The man had handed him another bunch of mums. He'd given Klein no indication he'd ever seen him before.

When Catherine had greeted him at the door, he'd made a show of the flowers, and kissed her. Then he'd complained of being tired and had run his bath.

He put on his pajamas and robe, and settled back in his chair to read further on the Red Shield. He remembered getting up and going to bed.

The Red Shield team arrives carrying placards and banners; they meet to decide his fate. It is pure anxiety as he waits in his office for the results.

He knows well enough what is coming! He is punched and pushed to the little park right in front of the State Department, just by the statue of the Greek discus thrower, which wouldn't be in a Chinese village. His students mill around—he can recognize some of them—how can they do it? He is stripped, splattered with black ink, has signs hung on him: CORRUPT ACADEMIC AUTHORITY, BLACK RESISTER, SNAKE DEMON. He recognizes Carolyn Carr in the crowd, but he won't reveal her. Carolyn comes toward him—his cock is inexplicably out—and melts right into him.

☆ ☆ ☆

Sansone finally picked up his papers and started home. He left a note that he'd be in a little late. The halls of the Department were slimy chalk.

Holmes plays an intricate game with a scissors and a needle and a beetle. The beetle is death, and the needle is . . . and the scissors is . . .

Anne opened the door. Sansone held himself up. "What a day!"

As the bombs fell, Smith had gotten away in his plane. Below he can see his own body, charred and broken. As he rises high over the earth, his hair is aflame with the sun!

THE THIRD DAY

Purple: Statement of the President of the United States for Delivery on National Television and Radio on December 9 at 11 a.m.

CONFIDENTIAL
(UNCLASSIFIED WHEN RELEASED)

Good morning. Since my talk to the American people two days ago, the crisis in Thailand has grown even more critical.

A Chinese Communist army has struck deeply, as much as 120 miles, into Thai territory, and has succeeded in overrunning a major American air base, at Udon Thani. The Communist Army has virtually no support from the Thai people.

The Thais are fighting in the defense of their homeland. In fulfillment of our treaty obligations, American air and ground units are fighting with them.

We are sending our troops into Thailand as fast as we can. But that is not enough. Heavily engaged as we are in Indochina and around the world, we cannot send in reinforcements as quickly as our troops need. Our forces are outnumbered ten and fifteen to one. Our brave boys are dying in Thailand, my fellow Americans, in such an unequal contest.

Two days ago, I made clear to the new leaders of Communist

China that unless their forces halted their advance into Thailand, I would authorize our troops to use tactical nuclear weapons by five p.m. today Washington time. The leaders of Communist China have not yet responded.

Yesterday at eleven ten a.m., the United States and Thailand accepted a cease-fire proposed by the Secretary General of the United Nations on the condition that the Chinese Communists do the same. Again, the leaders of Communist China have not responded.

Finally, at two thirty this morning, the United Nations Security Council endorsed a cease-fire in Thailand. Once more, the leaders of Communist China have not responded.

Time is running out. I do not wish to authorize the use of nuclear weapons. The idea of doing so weighs heavily on my mind. But a time is rapidly approaching when I may have to do so if the United States is to stand up to its responsibilities as the leader of the Free World.

The use of tactical nuclear weapons will not be without risks. In a desperate effort to continue their aggression in Thailand, the Chinese Communists have recently threatened American cities, should we attempt to stand up to them with these limited but powerful means of defense. To prevent our use of these weapons, they say they hold our cities at ransom.

To such threats, I say this: The American people will not be blackmailed. We have stood up to bullies before, and we will stand up to them now. The Free World is being tested in Thailand. It is a test we will not fail. Our strategic nuclear forces are on full alert. Any nuclear attack by Communist China against the United States or any of its allies will be met fifty to one.

I think the Chinese leaders fully understand this. They understand the total devastation which would be wreaked on their country should they make the insane choice of attempting to carry out their threats.

I appeal again to the leadership of Communist China not to force my hand. I pray that they may show wisdom at this critical hour.

My fellow Americans, please join me in praying for our brave *soldiers fighting, even now as I speak, in Thailand and in Indochina to defend freedom and peace.   Thank you.*

BLACK: US AIR FORCE FAR EASTERN COMMAND, DEC 9, 1220 HRS, FLASH IMMEDIATE (EYES ONLY THE PRESIDENT)

Q CLASSIFICATION

PREPARATIONS NOW RPT NOW COMPLETE FOR SIMULTANEOUS STRIKES ON CHICOM MISSILE FACILITIES AND STRATEGIC AIRFIELDS. FIRST MISSILE ATTACK WILL BE ON TAI LOU FACILITY AT 17:05 WASHINGTON TIME.

☆ ☆ ☆

Smith read through the new papers in his in-box. Who'd designed this fucking game anyway? He'd always hated those think-tank types who wore tweedy jackets and smoked pipes and luxuriated in dreams of probable disaster. Oh yes, they were necessary. He was willing, he supposed, to think the unthinkable, but he didn't have to like the cushy way they made their living at it.

He'd like to stick their noses in it, into the sheer horror of it. Spattered with blood, faces smashed, twisted metal, screams! It happened, yes, it happened, and when it did, it was the only thing in the world, even as you ran from it as fast as you could.

There was another cable in his in-box. He wouldn't read it.

☆ ☆ ☆

"If we start negotiating with the Chinese," Sansone told Tucker McGrath, "we'll do it through New York, right?"

"I hope you got some sleep, boss. You look terrible."

"I always sleep."

"You might want to take a look at the President's speech," Wylie Adams said. "It's appropriately bloody."

Sansone read it. "Okay, okay, but what I said still holds. The negotiations will be in New York, right at the UN."

"Which means," Tucker said, "that we better start putting together some instructions."

"You bet!" Sansone poked out the door, and called to Martha, "How about some sweet rolls for everyone, and two for me, okay?"

Carolyn Carr walked in. "Michael?"

He closed the door and kissed her.

"You seemed so cold last night. You made me feel like shit, you really did."

"I'm sorry. I just got a little funny."

"Because of your wife?"

"I guess so."

"Then maybe we shouldn't . . ."

He embraced her again.

"Do you really mean all this?"

"I do."

White: World Monitoring Service, Peking, December 9, 1900, Flash Transcription

OFFICIAL USE ONLY

Statement of Shih-Ying CHEN, Acting Chairman of the Central Committee of the People's Republic of China

President Murray threatens with nuclear weapons in Thailand, but he knows that he cannot use these weapons without sinking even further into the righteous hatred of all peace-loving peoples.

Before he takes the final step, the American President should think twice. The People's Republic of China is armed with a powerful nuclear arsenal of its own. Any nuclear blow against the People's Army will be met by instant retaliation.

The United States is accustomed to fighting wars in Asia, to killing and despoiling with no risks. Here is a war in which the big centers of capitalism will not be safe from the righteous retaliation of the peoples. San Francisco and Los Angeles could be the price of Mr. Murray's colonialist ventures. Those who survive will know whom to thank for the loss of their loved ones.

Purple: The NSC Committee on Southeast Asia will meet in the War Room of the Executive Office Building at 9:45 hours to discuss contingency plans relating to the present crisis.

Defense would have to talk about his conference now, Klein thought. He had the procedures, the site arrangements, the agenda all worked out as, at 7:45, he walked into the Secretary's preliminary meeting. Sansone brought notes on setting up tripartite talks in New York between the possible cochairmen. Holmes and Smith came in with nothing.

"Now's the time," Sansone said, "to get going on that conference."

"I suppose," the Secretary said, "New York might turn out to be the site, if events lead that way."

"Of course, it'll be in New York," Sansone said as if in an empty room. He gritted his teeth. The Secretary was so cool about the UN, but Sansone had to worry about it. Nobody was giving him any goddamn guidance. What the hell was he supposed to do?

They could ignore him for awhile, Klein thought, but sooner or later they'd all come to his conference. Well, wouldn't they?

Holmes smiled and said nothing. No, he would wait. He would be not the master detective, who must give an explanation, but rather the confidential butler who knows the answer but keeps his counsel.

For the meeting of the National Security Council, Defense had prepared a full set of briefings for the President. Mikesell outlined Air Force and Navy preparations for virtually simultaneous missile strikes on Chinese launch facilities and airfields. These would be followed up by B-52 raids. The aircraft had been en route all night from the United States and Europe to advance bases in Taiwan, Okinawa, and Vietnam. Interceptors were in readiness should any Chicom aircraft get through; ABM's were poised for the missiles. Finally, the entire Ballistic Missile System, including the nuclear submarine force, was on full alert.

Under Secretary Palmerston discussed the new environment which tactical nuclear weapons would create in Thailand. The Communists would be driven back—Defense had switched to the offensive—even with the inadequate numbers we now had. "We'll get back some of that real estate," General Curtis put in. "Perhaps all of it in a week to ten days."

Mikesell's shop had run studies on the likely train of events following the strikes. Liquidation of Chinese strategic capability, coupled with decisive use of tactical weapons, would quickly bring the Chinese to their senses. "We know using nuclear weapons is not altogether a popular course," he said, turning to the President, "but from the military standpoint, it's the one most likely to ensure success. And after that, Mr. President, you won't *need* to worry about popularity, I can assure you."

"I guess not," said the President. "Hell, maybe I've got nothing to worry about."

Smith closed his eyes. The scene was like some medieval

satyricon in which nobles and prostitutes had dressed up as monks and nuns to drink and fornicate. He clutched his purse and his sword; he'd fornicated like everyone else!

" . . . been taking a terrible beating," General Curtis was saying, "but I think tomorrow that trend is going to be reversed. I'm thinking of tomorrow, sir, in Thailand. Our troops will be getting authorization at just five o'clock, just about dawn."

The Secretary signaled to speak. "The other alternative—it is ten thirty-five, and I know," he said, glancing at the President, "you must leave shortly for your television appearance—is if the Chinese *accept* the cease-fire."

"It seems to me," Palmerston cut in, "that we have to look at the facts. Right now the Chinese are winning. They're not going to be convinced otherwise, Mr. Secretary, until they're hurt."

The Secretary glanced briefly at Holmes, then smiled. "How curious." He glanced at his watch. "Well, we might, with no loss of realism, at least plan for the possibility."

The Secretary, Holmes guessed, had arrived some time ago at where Holmes himself now stood. Vane was one of those severe, great-coated figures who maintain in their silence some sure distance between themselves and the curiosities which life offers to their view. What had the Secretary said to him: "It will be more interesting that way?"

But if he were right, Holmes mused, how would the American side ever use its nuclear weapons?

The Secretary continued almost playfully. "Today, the Chinese occupy Northern Thailand and no small part of Central Thailand as well. Why should they leave?"

"The war!" cried General Curtis. "They know we'll get them out of there if we have to incinerate every one of them! They'll leave. They're not that stupid. They're not going to tangle with us, not an American army armed with nukes and willing to use 'em, no sir!"

"I think you're right." The Secretary smiled.

Smith, looking at the President, suddenly said, "You gentlemen seem like sporting men. What kind of odds will you give me that Mitchell Murray will be the first President since Harry Truman to use nuclear weapons?"

Smith saw the President shake his head. What would he be thinking? "Where did they find this guy? He must be crazy. He'll never hold another post in the U.S. Government, not if Mitch Murray has anything to do with it." What did Smith care? There would be no sound, but a searing white flash burning out their eyes. Then the shock wave would be like the ocean, turning them over and over.

The President left to broadcast his statement. Sansone would have to send a statement to Kirkland. But what was he supposed to tell him? Again, they'd given him no guidelines. They'd completely cut him out. Him, Frank Sansone! What was the matter with those bastards? Next time he'd show 'em. He'd kick their balls in! Bastards! Bastards! Bastards!

So mad! What was he so mad about? He felt dizzy, then sick to his stomach. He made it to the john, then vomited, quick, staccato vomits more like coughs or hiccups. His chest ached.

It must have been the sweet rolls, he said to himself. He'd kind of liked them. They wouldn't sell a bad sweet roll, not here at State. He wiped his mouth with a piece of toilet paper. Nothing had gotten on his suit. He put the seat down and sat. He was shivering.

Did anyone know he was here?

He got up and headed back. He must look like hell. As he walked in, he said, "I think we'd better draft up a statement for Kirkland," and went into his office. He slouched back in his swivel chair.

Klein pondered: given the situation, did he want to take Carolyn Carr out to lunch? It was twelve o'clock before he asked her. "I'm going with someone else," she said in a purposive, wooden stage-voice that sought no further invitation. From his window, Klein spotted them as they walked through the parking lot. Wyzanski had his arm around her; she had a sexy way of moving her hips.

Sansone sat in his swivel chair, unwilling to move. He had best sit and wait.

"When you come down to it," he said to himself, "what's this game anyway? It's all been a fake. What does it matter?" But then he smiled. "It's had its moments though, like when I got everyone going, when they were all sitting around dead on their asses. I was the only one there with any balls, Anne. You would have been proud of me. God, with everything that's happened to me in the last few years, I don't know what I would have done without you. You're the only one who still believes in me. You'd have been proud of me, honey, even in a crazy-ass business like this."

On Smith's desk was still another scare statement by Chairman Chen.

Smith was outside lighting fires in the street. His staff was preparing another move on the Iran problem. They were back there in their game room with their game cables and their game studies, as if in a doll's house.

They floated, the paper dolls, in their candlelit baskets down the Potomac, as they had, after the first nuclear blast, down the river past Hiroshima!

Smith laughed to himself, and then the laughter caught and became hysterical, and then it passed, followed by an immense calm. He picked up the phone. "Control, this is J. Zachariah Smith, Assistant Secretary of State."

"What is your Control Number?"

"X67894."

"Your voice and number have been verified. You may proceed."

"I have been authorized by the President of the United States and the Secretary of State to send the following message without further clearance."

"No further clearances are required?"

"That is correct. The message is to R.V. Rogachev, Chairman, Council of Ministers, U.S.S.R."

"To R.V. Rogachev, Chairman, Council of Ministers, U.S.S.R."

"That is correct. The message is as follows: *The United States has already launched a massive strike against Chinese Communist missile facilities and airfields on mainland China.*" (Smith could hear the electronic hum as his message began its conversion into a telegram.) *"It is clear that your treaty obligations to the Chinese will require you to respond in kind against the United States. I have therefore authorized our Ballistic Missile System to eliminate all Soviet missile bases and airfields capable of launching an attack against the United States. Signed J. Zachariah Smith for the President."*

☆ ☆ ☆

PURPLE: DEC 9, 1650 HRS, FLASH IMMEDIATE, US USSR TELINE, EYES ONLY, CHAIRMAN ROGACHEV

TOP SECRET

FOLLOWING MESSAGE AUTHORIZED BY PRESIDENT USA:

THE UNITED STATES HAS ALREADY LAUNCHED A MASSIVE STRIKE AGAINST CHINESE COMMUNIST NUCLEAR FACILITIES AND AIRFIELDS ON MAINLAND CHINA...

Two minutes later, Henderson burst into his office. "Smith, Smith, what's the meaning of this?"

"Read it for yourself!"

"You're deliberately inviting the Soviets to attack us!"

Mitchell Murray entered, then Vane, Mikesell, General Curtis, Holmes, Klein.

Murray was saying, "For Christ sake, we're going to be in a war. It's bound to get out, and . . . it certainly won't look good for *me*!"

"It probably won't," Smith said.

Henderson bore down, "You've completely sabotaged the game, Smith. I'll write a full report on this!"

"Now you'll know it could happen."

"You're out! You're out!" Henderson screamed. "You'll have to resign from the Department."

"Yes, I think maybe you're right. I think it's time for me to retire."

"Traitor!"

Vane said, "Although I do not personally condone your action, Zach, I think you've shown us an interesting possibility." Vane turned to Mikesell and Curtis. "One's faith in reason should, at best, be fairly limited. I . . . Where is Senator Sansone? We were *all* called in here. Where's the Senator?"

Holmes volunteered, "I'll check at his office."

"Yes, get him in here."

"What good could *he* do?" Murray asked.

As Holmes walked into Sansone's office, he saw his huge hulk slumped into a chair. "Senator? Senator?" When he shook him, Sansone's body lurched forward. "He's dead!"

Tucker McGrath felt his pulse, then stood before the body as if he were holding his hat over his heart. "The boss is dead alright."

"He doesn't look dead," Martha said, beginning to cry, "but somehow I know he is."

When the others rushed in, Mikesell said that the Senator must have had a heart attack, and died without waking up.

Vane remarked, "I'm afraid the Senator took all this business much too seriously."

Smith exploded, "Now you've got a real body here. Call an ambulance, for Christ sake! Get him out of here! And then you can all go on playing the game. Go on, go on! Go on playing your goddamn game!"

When he returned to his office, Smith noticed two telegrams in his in-box.

BLUE: US MISSION UN, DEC 9, 1650 HRS, FLASH IMMEDIATE (PASS TO PRESIDENT)

OFFICIAL USE ONLY

CHINESE COMMUNISTS ISSUED FORMAL ACCEPTANCE CEASE FIRE.

BLUE: SATELLITE OBSERVATION READOUT CENTER, DEC 9, 1720 HRS

TOP SECRET

MASSIVE SOVIET MISSILE LAUNCH DETECTED.

☆ ☆ ☆

Of course, Holmes said to himself.

It was only the following September that he received an

announcement from Smith and his wife, Sally Jenks, of the birth of their daughter, Sarah.

Another real life had begun!

DATE DUE

5-23-03			
6-2-03			
7-7-03			
7-21-03			
8-28-03			
12-2-03			

DEMCO